BLAME IT ON THE BUGATTI

by

Trisha King

Published by New Generation Publishing in 2016

First Edition

www.newgeneration-publishing.com

New Generation Publishing

Chapter 1

The Contessa Aurelia di Tramonti woke from her second facelift with a mixture of apprehension and anticipation. That there would be pain, of course, she was well aware from her first experience: the sharp cuts and tender bruising, the swellings and stitches. She clung to the hope that techniques had improved in the past 10 years. But then again, she had requested more work this time – around the eyes and mouth especially. The pain would pass; she could bear it.

The real worry was the fear. Supposing the surgeon had made any mistakes – a little too much removed here, a little too much inserted there? She had paid for the finest specialist in Italy, but still, it was delicate work, requiring artistry as well as skill. The Contessa had a horror of emerging like one of those celebrities picked apart in magazines for the inept 'procedures' that had cost them so much money.

Too late to worry about all that now. Best to focus on the outcome. Always beautiful, the Contessa had maintained her figure by heroic bouts of self-denial plus the occasional clinical intervention, and she could still turn heads. But the face seemed to go its own way despite all one's best efforts, and the only solution was the most drastic one. Last time round it had been a triumph; she had been exultant. She so much wanted to have that feeling again.

The Contessa drifted in and out of sleep, sometimes aware of medical staff checking her blood pressure or the drip, but mostly blissfully wrapped in a warm cocoon of anaesthetics.

The next morning she was sitting up in bed, gingerly sipping water through a straw, and working out what time she would have to get dressed. As before, she insisted on Giancarlo taking her to the clinic, and collecting her afterwards. The clinic was very discreet, and it was unlikely she would be seen by anyone, but just in case she should run into someone who recognised her, she wanted to show that she was having work done with the full support of her husband, not sneaking in and hiding away for weeks the way some women did, in the craven hope of hanging onto their men.

Her mobile phone rang; it was Giancarlo: "Aurelia, I'm afraid I won't be able to pick you up. Some idiot drove right into me, and now I'm stuck on the motorway waiting to be towed away."

"But how will I get home?" the Contessa wailed.

As Giancarlo expected, his wife's first thought would be for her convenience, rather than his welfare. "I am unharmed – thank you for asking," he said. "And don't worry, I have arranged for a chauffeur and car to collect you from the clinic."

The Contessa sighed her resignation. Men were so unreliable. Though not a woman much given to humility, she did occasionally admit to herself that she had very poor taste in husbands. Her first had been wealthy, naturally, and more than twice her age, but had drunk himself to death before she had reached 30.

Still, he had left her the ancestral palazzo, and the collections; and the title. Though Italy was unable to field an actual monarch, it happily retained its noble appellations. Aurelia adored any association with the aristocracy; it added just that dash of class. Being addressed as Contessa certainly had the power to impress people, particularly the foreigners who seemed to constitute most of their acquaintances.

She had come across Giancarlo while enjoying her widowhood. He had been ravishingly handsome and charming, and she did not see why she should resist him. Giancarlo had professed himself to be a businessman, and made frequent trips away "buying and selling". Together they made a fine couple, and delighted in spending her money. From the start, Aurelia had taken the precaution of insisting that she had to give approval for any withdrawals from their joint account. He had complained that this was demeaning to a man and an insult to their love, but when he realised she wouldn't budge on the issue, he had to go along with it.

At 54 her husband was still remarkably good-looking. It was so unfair the way a sprinkling of silver hair and a few character lines seemed to age a woman while somehow enhancing a man. Obviously there had been other women along the way, but Giancarlo behaved with discretion, and publicly he always treated her with the utmost respect. As she grew older, she valued more and more having a steady consort, whose spending she could largely control.

Chapter 2

Late in the afternoon, and swathed in scarves and dark glasses, she emerged from the limousine and swept past the chauffeur without a glance.

The house was mercifully quiet. Leaving her case for Josefina to unpack later, the Contessa went straight to her bedroom to peer at her face in the mirror. Though prepared for the sight that confronted her, it still took her breath away: dark stitches, eyes almost closed like a boxer's, mouth swollen and bruised. She sat on the bed; she must have courage – these things would disappear over time, and she would surely be left with ...

Her phone rang. It would be Giancarlo. "So, you are home safe and sound."

"Where are you, Giancarlo? I thought you would be back by now. Josefina is nowhere in sight, and I need someone to make me some herbal tea."

Giancarlo closed his eyes as his wife ranted on – whining hag! Mean and selfish. Well, she'd see. "Aurelia, shut up and sit down!"

Aurelia stopped in mid-sentence and flopped into the nearest chair. They had had some spectacular fights in the past, but of late he had rarely raised his voice to her.

Giancarlo imagined her sitting in her bedroom, shocked and perplexed. He felt exhilarated by his sudden power. "That's better. Now, I have something to tell you." He paused for dramatic effect. "I'm leaving you." Her hand flew to her face, and she winced as she touched the tender

4

flesh. He heard her gasp. "In fact, I have already left you."

"But why?" she wailed in a small voice.

"Why? Because I cannot endure living with you a single moment longer. I am so tired of your controlling and your complaining, and I can hardly bear to be in the same room as you." My God, this felt good! He should have done it years ago.

"Controlling!" she snorted. She was beginning to get her spirits back. "When you are never here – how on earth could I be accused of controlling you? And as for 'complaining'. I put up with your endless parade of women – which I never mention. Your pathetic business ventures – which I never mention. Your embarrassing attempts to ingratiate yourself with my diplomatic friends – which I never mention."

He could picture her pacing round the room, working herself up. "You control the purse strings" he said. "You always have and you always will, and I find it intolerable."

"Ah, ha, ha," she almost laughed. "Now we're getting to it. Now the great Giancarlo, the charming Giancarlo, is showing himself for the money-grubbing little leech he has always been! If I hadn't 'controlled' your reckless spending we would have nothing left by now, we would be living on bread and water. Well, allow me to point out that you won't get a penny more out of me. See how long you last on that before you come crawling back, begging my forgiveness."

Giancarlo lit a cigarette and inhaled deeply. His silence unnerved her. She had a sudden thought, and rushed to her bureau. He could hear her rummaging about in the drawers and compartments. Then the little sigh of relief

5

when she found what she was looking for. God, she was so predictable. "Did you think I'd stolen your jewellery?"

"I think you would stoop to anything. You've made it perfectly clear that you have resented me for years, simply because I behave like a responsible adult, while you're nothing but a spoilt brat. You're not 25 any longer, Giancarlo. And no doubt you've got some bimbo in tow. Well, how long do you imagine she'll stick around when you've run out of money?"

"Oh, I won't run out of money – you can be sure of that."

Once again, she was unnerved – this time by his self-assurance. He had always had an easy charm, which could seem to others like self-confidence. But she knew it to be a façade. She stood perfectly still. "Don't tell me one of your grand schemes has actually paid off? That would be a first!"

"Not only has it paid off," he laughed, "it will continue to pay off. And I have you to thank for it."

Aurelia's memory searched frantically to recall what madcap ventures her husband had been involved in lately. She usually took little notice, except when he wanted money. But nothing significant came to mind. "Well?" she said. "Astonish me! How do you propose to earn your living without my support?"

Giancarlo laughed softly. "My dear Aurelia, have you looked around you?"

She looked up, turning this way and that, scanning the room for clues. Everything seemed to be as it was. Then she spun round. Something was missing. A small painting, a favourite of hers, was no longer in its place. There was just a rectangular patch where the painting

6

should have been. "My 'Madonna and Child'!" she cried. "You've taken it!"

He said nothing. At which she raced into the hallway. There were a few gaps on the walls there, too. "Bastardo!" she spat. Again, he did not respond. She ran downstairs to the drawing room, the dining room, the old ballroom, the library. Everywhere she looked there were patches on the walls. But more than that, other precious items were missing: silverware, gilt mirrors, tapestries, crystal candelabra, ornamental clocks, the rare medieval books – all gone. "You bastard!" she repeated.

Giancarlo was quite calm. "Now do you see how I will 'manage to live'?" he taunted. "And I have you to thank for the idea," he repeated.

"Me?"

"Yes indeed. Remember when you decided to buy the Bugatti?" That Bugatti had been her pride and joy. She had toyed with the idea of spraying it pink, but Giancarlo was horrified, insisting it would be an abomination to impose pink on such a car. "It was the same year you planned your first little trip to the most expensive plastic surgeon in Italy. Then there were all those repairs when the roof leaked. And you were wondering how to pay for it all?"

She did remember, of course. The leak had damaged some of the frames that held the oldest paintings. An acquaintance had recommended a restorer, who had casually remarked on the value of the paintings: "I do hope you are properly insured, signora". Signora! Not even Contessa! She remembered that all right. She had sacked him and hired another restorer. She also decided to sell her least favourite painting, and found a dealer who sold it to a private client. The painting not only paid for the

7

beautiful Bugatti, it left over a considerable amount to be invested elsewhere. Husband and wife had laughed at their good fortune over a bottle of champagne from the cellars. The cellars!

"No doubt you have raided the cellars, too?" she spat. "You won't get away with this!"

"Oh Aurelia, such a cliché. You've been watching too many films."

"I will call the police and tell them what you've done," she said.

"You will not call the police, Aurelia. You will do nothing for the next two hours."

"And what's to stop me? You certainly don't scare me."

"Oh I am far away. However, my ... associate is watching you now. If you call anyone, go anywhere within the next two hours, he has his instructions."

"To do what?"

"In the circumstances, I have been remarkably generous, Aurelia. I have left you your car, your jewels, most of the wine cellar, a few trinkets I don't particularly want. They will fund your life for a while. But if you contact anyone within the next two hours, those things will be taken from you by a man who is not as, shall we say, sensitive as I am."

"I'm not afraid of you or your associates."

"You should be," he responded, and disconnected the call.

The Contessa sank into the nearest chair to catch her breath, and to brood.

Chapter 3

Giancarlo waited among the trees outside the house, and gave silent thanks to the Bugatti. Finding themselves in a position to go out one day and simply buy a Bugatti had changed everything. For the first time it brought home to them how much ready cash surrounded them in the form of saleable artefacts. He had loved that car. Aurelia always referred to it as 'my Bugatti', but whenever he drove it he felt like a maharajah. Years later, they were both a little sad to see it go, but were soon consoled by their new vehicles.

He glanced at the palazzo. Giancarlo knew his wife to be impulsive: if she was going to do something, she would do it right away. 20 minutes passed without any movement. Well, he must have really knocked the wind out of her sails this time.

He smiled to himself as he switched on the battered Fiat's ignition. The car had its share of dents and scratches, and the inside obviously hadn't been cleaned for months. No matter. After a few miles he came to the lake near the woods, and took a walk. There was no-one around. But just in case, he picked up a handful of large pebbles and threw them as far as he could into the water one by one. On his fifth throw, the pay-as-you-go mobile phone sailed through the air, and he heard its satisfying 'plop' as it hit the deep water. He threw a few more stones and then, seemingly bored with the game, he sauntered back to the car and drove off.

The road wound steadily upwards for several miles. He pulled off the main road onto a narrower lane, and climbed higher still. Dusk was beginning to fall as the track twisted and turned back on itself. There was little traffic about. Eventually, he drew into a small lay-by. During the day, it afforded spectacular views across the valley to the distant mountains. A van was parked there, the driver leaning on the rail, contemplating the slowly-fading hills.

Giancarlo stepped out of the car and greeted him, "Ciao, Fredo".

Fredo drew on a cigarette and grunted a greeting. There was no shaking of hands. Though a head shorter than Giancarlo, Fredo was a powerfully-built man who exuded menace. He moved to the back of the van and opened the doors. Giancarlo peered inside. Everything looked just as he'd left it: racks holding paintings wrapped in blankets and cloths, boxes of crystal and silverware cushioned in bubble-wrap, rolled carpets and tapestries.

Though there was no specific reason to distrust Fredo, Giancarlo had taken the precaution of putting tiny marks on the backs of the items, and looked for them now. Fredo watched this pantomime in simmering silence, smoking his cigarette, thinking: *I don't want your precious paintings; they're no good to me. How would I get rid of them without a whole heap of trouble? I just want your money, and to get out of here quick. And if you give me any grief, I will slit your throat and take your money anyway.*

"Did she get a good look at you, when you picked her up?" asked Giancarlo.

"Didn't even notice me," Fredo replied. "Just in case, I was wearing a chauffeur's peaked cap and dark glasses. But they weren't necessary. I was no different from a piece of furniture in her eyes."

Satisfied, Giancarlo closed the van doors. He reached into his overcoat and brought out a thick envelope. "Used

Euros - as agreed," he said. Fredo took the packet, swiftly flicked through the notes inside, and put the envelope in his pocket with one hand. With the other, he held out the keys to the van. Giancarlo took them, and passed the Fiat keys to Fredo. Their gloved hands touched; it was their only physical contact.

"Maybe you can buy a new car," said Giancarlo. "Or at least, have this one cleaned." Fredo snorted and turned away. He hoped never to see this smarmy man again. And his wish came true, for at Fredo's turn Giancarlo reached once more into his overcoat, pulled out the stun gun, and fired it into Fredo's neck. He went down like an ox. The internet was a wonderful thing; you could buy anything you wanted.

Quickly, Giancarlo bent and retrieved the keys from Fredo's hand, and the envelope from his pocket. No sense in wasting good money. He then dragged the limp Fredo to the rail, struggled to lift his heavy torso up the bars, and just managed to push him over the edge. It was a long way down. Giancarlo could neither see nor hear the landing, but he was confident he wouldn't be troubled by Fredo ever again.

Panting from the exertion, he got into Fredo's Fiat and re-parked it at an awkward angle, as if in a hurry. He left the keys in the ignition and the driver's door open. They may never find Fredo's body, but they would certainly find his car, so the scene had to look like a man driving erratically, who'd jumped out of the car, climbed the rail and flung himself into the unknown. For what reason? Who could say? Such cases are all very sad, but unfathomable.

Giancarlo climbed into the van, turned the key, and drove off into the dusk.

Chapter 4

The Contessa sat with a glass of vodka and tonic, and
thought through her options. There was no sign of
Josefina. Giancarlo must have got her out of the house on
some pretext so he could steal her things. Well, they had
originally been her first husband's things, in the family for
generations. But since the Conte's death, she had come to
regard them with something of a proprietorial air, as
though they had been in *her* family for generations, and
she was incensed that Giancarlo could even begin to
imagine he had any right to take them. One thing was
clear: she would not let him get away with it.

Even to herself, this sounded like a line from a cheap
book. Aurelia shook her head, and groaned with pain. So
shocked by this sudden turn of events, she had all but
forgotten the bruising and swelling on her face. The
painkillers must be wearing off. Fumbling in her handbag,
she swallowed more pills. She had to focus, to plan. She
had been a resourceful young woman and had used her
attributes to create her own chances, plucking a beautiful
life off the tree like a ripe plum. Then, as now,
circumstances had forced her hand. She had done it
before; there was no reason why she couldn't do it again.
And in the process, she would drag down her selfish,
useless husband.

Gradually, ideas fell into place; a strategy began to take
shape. She was supposed to do nothing for two hours, or
else. She dismissed this as fantasy. Even if someone was
watching from the road, which she very much doubted,
they couldn't possibly see into the house itself. Draining
her second glass, Aurelia went into her dressing room and
took down a small case. She rummaged among her shoes,
several pairs still in their boxes. Giancarlo had seen them

once, and remarked on the profligacy of a woman who could buy so many shoes that never even saw the light of day. She took off various lids, revealing court shoes, towering stilettos and sparkly sandals, all stuffed with tissues to keep their shape. Carefully, she pulled out the tissues and unrolled the flimsy paper. Each contained a wad of notes. *You believe you're so clever, Giancarlo, but you didn't know about this, did you?* Stuffing the money into the case, she pushed the tissues back in the shoes and replaced the lids.

Moving on to her bureau, she tipped the drawers of jewels into her case, leaving the empty containers lying about the floor. She opened the safe. It was odd that he had taken nothing from the safe. Perhaps he thought he didn't need anything from it, given everything else he had. She scooped all the contents into the case and left the safe door conspicuously open. Then, she packed the few things she would need, and stopped only when the case couldn't take any more. It was heavy, but manageable. She carried it down to the cellar, wondering what havoc Giancarlo had wreaked there. But again, she was surprised: he really had taken only a few bottles. All the most precious wine remained lying there, nestled among straw and years of cobwebs. Good. She pushed the case into a bin and covered it with straw.

Chapter 5

Though he had lived in the little town for over two years, Officer Paulo had never seen the Contessa close-to. Of course, she was a familiar figure driving about in her beautiful, powder blue Lamborghini. As was the husband in his glistening red Ferrari. What a car that was! How all the young men sighed when they saw it speed by. They ached to own such a car themselves; it was almost a physical pain.

Silhouetted in the open doorway of the house, the Contessa looked, to Paulo, just like a 1960s film star: the long, slender legs, the curvy figure, black cigarette held delicately aloft. She must be in her 50s, but she was still a stunner. Her head was draped in a silk scarf that almost covered her face, and even in the fading light she wore large sunglasses.

"Contessa," he smiled, with a slight bow. He was young and quite good-looking, and she thought: *You'll do nicely.* He started to introduce himself, but she waved that aside imperiously: "I know who you are, Sergeant. Don't forget, I asked for you personally". Paulo wondered how she knew whom to ask for, since they had never met.

"I am merely a humble Officer, Contessa."

"Yes, yes, Sergeant. Come in."

They sat down, and as she drew on her cigarette, he noticed that her mouth seemed a little swollen.

"Now, I need you to be discreet," she said. "That's why I asked for you personally. This is a very delicate matter, Sergeant."

Throughout their conversation the Contessa continued to address him as Sergeant. He corrected her several times, but in the end he gave in – why not? It felt good to be called Sergeant.

The Contessa explained that she had been away for a few days and, returning home earlier than planned, had come across her husband loading a painting into a lorry. When asked what on earth he was doing, he announced that he was leaving her immediately. Behind him, she could see that the vehicle was stacked with paintings and boxes, and she rushed into the house. Everywhere she looked, it was clear that things were missing, valuable things. Her husband followed her inside, and continued to lift paintings off the wall. She accused him of taking leave of his senses, and demanded he return her property at once, or she would call the police.

"That was when he turned nasty," she said, whipping off her sunglasses to dab away the tears, before swiftly putting them back on again. But Paulo had seen the two black, nearly-closed eyes. She took another draw on her cigarette, wincing with the pain of moving her puffy lips. Paulo carefully wrote it all down in his notebook.

"He threatened that if I called the police, he would come back and get me. He has always had a violent temper, though only I know about that, as he is usually careful to hide it from others."

She led Paulo from room to room, indicating what was missing, while he noted down what he saw: gaps on the walls, display cases in disarray, the empty jewel boxes, the open door of the safe.

"I wanted you to see all this right away, Sergeant," she said. "But now I feel a little tired." Her hand trembled slightly as she lifted the cigarette once more to her mouth.

"Are you alone in the house, Contessa?" he asked with concern.

"We have staff: my maid Josefina, gardeners, others." She waved an airy hand; Contessas should not be expected to know how many staff they have. "I imagine my husband got them out of the way so that he could steal my possessions without being disturbed."

"You must not stay here by yourself tonight, Contessa, in case he comes back."

"I have no intention of staying here tonight. I will go to Josefina's. No doubt you will return tomorrow?"

"Yes, Contessa. It will be necessary to make a full list of everything that has been taken. And, of course, to take fingerprints."

"Fingerprints? Why would you need to take fingerprints? I have told you what happened; who took my things." He was aware that she had stopped calling him 'Sergeant'.

"It is just procedure, Contessa. We have to do it in all cases of burglary."

She sighed. "Very well. When I return from Josefina's in the morning, I will ring you to arrange to let you in so that you can do your work. You will come alone?"

"In the morning, yes. But my superiors will undoubtedly arrange for a forensic team to arrive later in the day, or possibly early the next day. I must ask you not to touch anything until they have done their work."

"I understand. But please, Sergeant, may I urge you to keep this matter to yourself tonight. I don't want all and sundry coming round here, gawping. By the time I have had a night's sleep at Josefina's I will feel able to face whatever has to be done."

"Of course, Contessa. You can depend on my discretion. " The little bow again. "Good evening."

Chapter 6

Giancarlo sat in a crowded bar in Milan, sipping a small beer. All eyes were on the large screen that dominated one wall, watching their idols playing the Neapolitan posers. The partisan crowd shouted advice to their own footballers, and heaped abuse on their age-old rivals from the south. The eyesight and parentage of the referee and line judges were called into question, depending on their decisions. Being the semi-final, it was a match that must be won, and it demanded intense concentration and commitment from everyone there.

Giancarlo looked at the screen, but his mind slid back to the house, wondering what his wife would be doing right now. She may be impulsive, but she was not stupid. In taking her valuables, he knew he had struck her to the core, and no matter if her instincts told her to do something, anything, to vent her feelings, she would have enough self-control to think through her options.

It wasn't as if he'd left her destitute – that would have been counter-productive, since it would certainly have provoked a wild, vindictive response. He had left money in the safe, boxes of jewellery, the largest paintings, her fancy car. And he had hardly touched the cellar, mostly because of the difficulty of transporting the bottles without damaging their contents. There was always the house, of course, although he knew she would rather die than sell the house, which made such a pretty backdrop to her aristocratic title.

Yes, she had plenty of assets, and these would keep her going for a considerable time. Perhaps, with her new face, she might try pitching for one of the ageing millionaires who seemed to gravitate to the parties in the city. It would be a good trade-off: he would gain some class to make his money look more respectable, and she would secure the wealth she loved. Yes, this would be an excellent option for her.

She might try to claim off the insurance for the missing items, but this would mean involving the police, who would soon discover that there was no sign of a break-in, no fingerprints other than those that should have been there. Inevitably, it would become clear that this was some sort of domestic dispute that had, perhaps, gone a little further than most. He was confident Aurelia would want, at all costs, to avoid the embarrassment of having to publicly admit that her 'dear Giancarlo' despised her enough to walk out and take her treasures with him. This would be beyond endurance for someone of Aurelia's pride.

No, her best strategy would be to sit tight, tell people that her beloved husband was on an extended overseas trip setting up a new business, make up some story for the few staff who would notice the missing items, and carry on as normal while her face healed and she could start her fishing expedition.

The crowd in the bar roared a collective groan, which jolted his attention back to the screen. The Neapolitans had scored a goal. He glanced round the room. It had filled considerably since the game started. People were gesticulating excitedly at the screen, cursing the despised southerners. With just 10 minutes left of the match, Giancarlo stood up and made his way through the door leading to the toilets.

The Gents looked deserted, and he stood at the sink as if drying his hands. The door opened, and a young-ish man walked in. Giancarlo had never seen him before. He looked at Giancarlo in the mirror. The man handed a small package to Giancarlo, who took it and immediately went into a cubicle and locked the door. Inside the package were a passport and driving licence. Giancarlo opened up the passport. The picture was his, the date of birth was a couple of years out, and the name listed was completely different. So, he was to be known as Massio Maggiore. Good.

Giancarlo, who was now Massio, left the cubicle. The man was standing at a urinal. Giancarlo stood next to him, and handed him an envelope. The man opened it swiftly, delved inside, nodded, and left. The whole process had taken only a few minutes.

Giancarlo returned to his table in the bar, and resumed sipping his beer while watching the screen. Thankfully, from his point of view, there were no more goals. No need for extra time or penalty shoot-outs; a clear win for the Neapolitans. Having nothing to celebrate, the downcast crowd finished their drinks and began drifting away. Giancarlo, who was now Massio, among them.

He drove the second-hand 4-wheel drive back to the rented lock-up and reversed it up to the rear of the van parked inside. Carefully, he transferred some of the paintings and boxes from the van to the car. Mm. Clearly, it was going to take several trips to move everything. Well, no matter. He had a new identity, a new car, and there was nothing to connect him with Giancarlo di Tramonti, the Contessa's husband. He packed out the back of the car with the tent, duvets, beach towels, all the camping paraphernalia he had bought in advance, and drove off into the night. If stopped, he would be just another holidaymaker.

Chapter 7

As soon as the lights of the young policeman's car faded from view, the Contessa locked the front door from the inside, leaving the keys in the lock as she usually did. She insisted on leaving keys in prominent places all over the house. A succession of Josefinas had warned her many times that this was not a good idea, but she had a horror of being trapped inside by a fire and not being able to find the keys to get out, and in the end the Josefinas had merely shrugged and let her get on with it.

She quickly checked all the rooms, trying to see them with a stranger's eyes, then hurried down to the cellar and retrieved her case, being careful to pull the straw back in place.

The key ring hung in its usual place next to the kitchen door. Wrapping a scarf around her hand, she picked up the key together with the pasta tongs that were lying on the draining board. Once outside, she locked the door. Balancing on an old garden chair, she looped the key ring round the tongs, leaned in through the little top window and hooked the key ring back in place, dropping the tongs on the draining board. She pushed the window closed with her knuckles, heard the satisfying click shut, and replaced the chair. It was ridiculously easy, a trick she had been taught by her brother when she was seven years old. Someone would work it out eventually, of course, but meanwhile it bought precious time.

Picking up her case, the Contessa walked round the side of the house to the garage block. Her husband's Ferrari was nowhere to be seen, naturally. But what was known as the 'family car', a sturdy Mercedes-Benz available to either of them, waited patiently in the garage for a run out. It hadn't been used for quite a while, but the engine started first time. Loading her case into the boot, the Contessa backed out and closed the garage door, but did not lock it. She drove past the greenhouses, out of the tradesmen's entrance, and headed south.

Chapter 8

Giancarlo, who was now Massio, made good progress. The car's cargo was too precious to risk driving fast, but he steadily clocked up the kilometres as he headed towards the border. Besides, it was better not to draw attention to himself.

Though late at night, a surprising number of vehicles waited to cross. There was the usual melee of guards and sniffer dogs moving around the cars and lorries, while people got out and stretched their legs as their passports were checked. The customs guards seemed to show particular interest in foreign vehicles, especially those with young male occupants, but when it was Giancarlo's turn, he was waved through without incident.

He drove on for an hour or so into France, then pulled off the road to find a quiet lay-by for a few hours sleep.

At the other end of Italy, the Contessa, who was still a Contessa, parked the Mercedes in a side street, pulled the scarf around her face, put on her dark glasses, and made her way to the busy bars that ringed the port. She knew what port towns were like; she had grown up in one when her name was Maria, and had made a point of avoiding them for more than 30 years. She had never been to this particular place before, but of one thing she was certain: port towns are the same the world over, and so are the men who live and work in them.

It didn't take long to find what she was looking for. Less than two hours later, with the Contessa and her case safely on board, the shabby boat headed out across the Adriatic.

Climbing off the boat, the Contessa saw car lights coming towards them, and a non-descript vehicle drew up. The pilot and the driver greeted each other, both drawing on the stubs of cigarettes while they held a brief conversation. Then the pilot held out his hand to her. She thought for a moment that he wanted to shake her hand, but the angle of his arm wasn't quite right for that. She handed him the keys to the Mercedes, he climbed back into the boat and sped off. Within hours, the Mercedes would have new number plates, and be on sale to people who don't ask too many questions.

Her driver didn't speak for the whole journey, which was just as well because she didn't understand his language. It was light by the time they arrived at the airport. From the back seat of the car, she handed him a wadge of notes, which he carefully counted. As she wheeled her case into the Departures lounge, the car sped away.

Chapter 9

By 11 a.m., the young Officer had still not heard from the Contessa. She would have been very tired and shaken, of course, and she was no spring chicken, so would need a good long sleep. He decided to wait one more hour before ringing her. He rang at 12.00, and again at 12.15. Then he got in his car.

The unmistakable powder blue Lamborghini hadn't moved from its place. There was no response when he rang the front door bell, so he walked all round the house. Everything was shut up. He got back into his car and drove to the village.

A few enquiries led him to Josefina's house. No, she hadn't heard from the Contessa last night, and she wasn't expecting to. The Contessa had left for a short holiday a few days ago, and her husband had given all the staff a week off on full pay. He was always generous, much more than her. Was there a problem? The policeman said there had been reports of a possible robbery at the house, and Josefina was to accompany him there, with her keys. Josefina's husband, Giuseppe, insisted on going with them, though whether that was out of protectiveness or curiosity wasn't clear. In his eagerness, Giuseppe forgot to remove the dinner napkin tucked into his shirt collar, and it flapped about, bearing the evidence of his abandoned meal.

When they reached the house, the policeman was surprised that Josefina walked past the front door and headed round the back towards the kitchen. "I don't have keys for the front door," she explained. "She doesn't like any of us to use it. All the staff have to come and go at the back of the house."

Once inside, Josefina called out a few times and, getting no reply, went upstairs to the Contessa's bedroom, the most likely place to find her. She let out a small scream, prompting her husband and the policeman to run up the stairs.

"There's been a break-in," she said, surveying the upheaval all about her. She picked up the jewellery boxes. "Her jewels – all gone." Her husband noticed the open safe door, and put his hand inside to see if anything was left. "Empty," he said.

"Don't touch anything," shouted Officer Paulo. "This is a crime scene."

"The collections," cried Josefina. At which Josefina and Giuseppe dashed downstairs, each darting into separate rooms, and shouting out what was missing. The policeman ran after first one, then the other, pleading in vain for them stay out of the rooms, not to touch anything. But they were unstoppable in their excitement. In desperation, he took out his gun and threatened to shoot them both if they didn't stand completely still! At once! That got their attention. Herding them into the kitchen, and telling them not to move a muscle until he returned, he quickly looked from room to room to make absolutely sure the Contessa was not there.

Then, with great trepidation, he made the phone call to his superior that he should have made the day before.

Chapter 10

Giancarlo/Massio took the motorway that skirted the Cote d'Azur. His was just another car travelling along the coast, keeping to the speed limit, and stopping now and again for food and petrol. There was the unavoidable detour round the Camargue before hugging the coast once again as the road turned south. He made good progress to the Spanish border, where again he was waved through without incident, and carried on southwards.

He was hot and tired by the time he reached the block of holiday apartments on the outskirts of Barcelona. He had chosen this block because it had an underground car park with a lift, and was inhabited by a changing population of tourists. He ate a meal, and sank onto the bed for a night's sleep.

The next day it took more than two hours to move everything from the car into the apartment he had rented on a short let, and was glad he had taken the precaution of buying a strong trolley to carry the big, heavy pictures. He had put on a pair of overalls and a baseball cap, and when the occasional resident entered the car park, they saw what looked like a deliveryman transporting boxes and pictures in bubble wrap to one of the flats.

At siesta time, he drove the empty car to a busy street, left the keys in the ignition, and walked away, confident that it would be stolen before the day was over. Late in the evening, he took a stroll to a little restaurant he'd seen earlier, and was delighted to note that the space where he'd left the car was now occupied by a small Seat.

He'd done it! There was no longer anything to connect him to Giancarlo. Tomorrow he would buy a new car, a

Spanish car. It had been a real wrench selling the Ferrari, the finest car ever made in his opinion. His wife would never imagine him parting from it. If she sent someone to try and find him, she would tell them to look for a red Ferrari. Well, he'd surprised her several times in the last few days, and he would do so again.

She had also been wrong about him having a bimbo in tow. He had never intended to take a girlfriend with him; that would have been far too risky. Better by far to set up his new life first. With his looks and the money from the sale of a painting or two, he would have no trouble attracting a beautiful young woman. And when she started making unreasonable demands, as they all did sooner or later, he would simply ditch her and find another.

No, the Ferrari was a car made to stand out from the crowd, and he did not need that kind of attention. He would drive only Spanish cars from now on. Besides, the cash from the Ferrari sale had paid for many things, and tomorrow it would buy him a new vehicle.

Chapter 11

The Contessa Aurelia made straight for the Ladies in the Departures lounge. Once inside a cubicle, she took out a mirror, slipped off her glasses and scarf, and examined her face against her passport photo. Oh. It was possible that they would not believe she was the woman in the passport. Even if they did, they would surely remember spending time examining her bruised face and her photo, looking for points of comparison. Better not to take that chance.

The scarf and glasses replaced, the Contessa pulled her case onto the escalator and walked across the concourse towards the Arrivals lounge. Standing back a little from the families and cab drivers hanging round the barrier, she waited until the next flight disgorged its passengers, mingled with the throng, and pulled her case out to a taxi rank, for all the world as though she had just landed.

Once deposited in a large tourist hotel, she ordered drinks with plenty of ice, using towels to turn them into ice packs for her swollen face. She remained in her room, studying flights between bouts of lying on the bed to let the ice do its work. A few days later, with the bruises receding and with some carefully applied make-up, she took a taxi back to the airport, and boarded her flight.

Chapter 12

The woman's voice thundered down the phone. "And this happened when? Yesterday?"

"Yes, Sir. Ma'am," he stumbled, almost dropping the telephone.

"And you thought it would be a really good idea to wait till today before reporting it?"

"You see, nothing really happened yesterday, and she asked me to wait"

"Stop wittering, man, and answer a simple question: did you deliberately delay reporting this incident?"

"Yes, Sir. Ma'am"

"And stop calling me Sir/Ma'am"

"Yes, Si ... Ma'am."

Officer Paulo had heard that there was a female Sergeant seconded to the district, but he hadn't expected her to pick up the phone. He knew when he made the call that he would be in trouble, so he was nervous to begin with. He had never worked for a woman before, and this, together with her abrupt manner, flustered him.

"I'm coming over."

Paulo waited anxiously at the front door when her car swept up the drive and she emerged onto the gravel. Sergeant Sylvia surveyed the outside of the house, while Paulo surveyed the outside of Sergeant Sylvia. She was quite old, perhaps in her early 40s, startlingly dyed yellow hair with black roots (his wife disapproved of black roots), jacket pulled tight across her ample bosom. He looked for a wedding ring, but failed to find one.

Not bothering to greet him, she marched into the hall, looking into each room and asking questions as he trailed behind her.

"Tell me exactly what happened yesterday."

"Well, Ma'am," he began, "the Contessa telephoned me in the early evening and asked me to come here at once as there had been an incident. When I arrived she seemed very upset. She told me that, on her return from a few days away, she found her husband loading paintings and other valuable items into a lorry. When she asked what he was doing, he said he was leaving her. She accused him of stealing her possessions and said she would call the police, at which point he threatened her."

She charged along the corridor. "What was the nature of this threat?"

"The husband said that if she contacted the police, he would come back and she'd be sorry. She stood up to him, and he attacked her, before driving away."

Sergeant Sylvia stopped dead in her tracks and turned to face Paulo, who had to brake hard to avoid bumping into her. "Attacked her? Did you see any evidence?"

"Certainly I did. Her face was bruised, her lips were cut and swollen and she had two black eyes."

"Anything else?"

"She looked frightened, she had been drinking, and her hand trembled as she smoked cigarettes. I wrote it all down in my notebook."

Sergeant Sylvia grunted; at least the young policeman had followed some procedures. She resumed her inspection of the rooms. "What happened next?"

"The Contessa took me round all the rooms and told me what was missing."

Sergeant Sylvia stopped again. "What I'm struggling to understand, officer, is that you came to the scene of a crime, the victim had been physically attacked and was here on her own, and yet you decided this was not sufficiently important to report for almost 20 hours."

"I intended to report it right away but she begged me not to. She said she was going to stay at her maid's house for the night, and would feel much more able to face the investigation once she'd had a night's sleep and a chance to pull herself together."

"This maid. Why wasn't she here yesterday? In fact, why are there no staff here now?"

"The maid, Josefina, told me that the husband had given all the staff a week's paid leave shortly after the Contessa had left on her trip."

"Interesting," she said, as they climbed the grand staircase. "Go on."

"This morning I was waiting for the Contessa to ring me, and when she didn't call, I rang the house a couple of times. There was no reply, so I drove over."

"What time was this?"

Paulo consulted his notebook. "I arrived here at 12.45. I rang the bell, I walked all round the house, but it was completely locked up with no sign of anyone."

"So how did you gain access? I assume you didn't break down a door?"

"No, Ma'am. I drove to the village and asked around for a Josefina who worked at the big house. When I located Josefina, I told her to bring her keys and come with me to the house. When we got inside we found all the doors had been locked from the inside, yet there was no sign of the Contessa."

"Did you check each room?"

"Yes, Ma'am."

"By yourself?"

"Well," he stared at his notebook to avoid looking at the Sergeant. "I checked downstairs, while they checked upstairs."

"They?"

"Josefina's husband had insisted on accompanying her."

"Officer, tell me you didn't let two civilians go into rooms by themselves; rooms that are crime scenes, that could have contained a body or an attacker."

"They rushed in before I could prevent them," he said sheepishly. "I realised they might contaminate evidence, but they just wouldn't listen. In the end I had to take drastic action to get their attention."

"Drastic action?"

"I threatened to shoot them unless they went back in the kitchen."

Sergeant Sylvia stared at him aghast. "You are telling me that you used your gun to threaten two members of the public, a gun that should never be drawn except in extreme circumstances?"

"I'm sorry, Ma'am. I didn't know what else to do, how to stop them touching evidence. I would never have actually shot them."

"No doubt that would be a great comfort to them as they passed out from a heart attack" she snorted.

Paulo's face and neck flushed, and he trailed miserably behind her as she returned to the front door.

"What will happen now, Sergeant?" He meant what will happen to me, but she chose to interpret his question differently.

Sergeant Sylvia took out her phone and started pressing buttons: "I call in the fingerprint team, and when they have completed their work I will organise a complete search of the property, inside and out."

"When will you ring the Inspector?"

"That depends on what the search party finds," she replied.

There was a pause. "Do you think he's killed her?" asked Paulo.

But she moved towards her car, barking instructions into the phone.

Chapter 13

Sitting on the terrace of a small bar in a little town perched high on a hill, Giancarlo sipped his coffee. It was not as good as Italian coffee, of course; but it was good enough. The sky was that radiant blue to be found most of the year in this part of Spain, heralding endless hot days. He gazed across the greenest of valleys and hillsides, and beyond to the sparkling Mediterranean. Birds swooped high over the lemon groves and the tiers of peach trees, and there was the faint sound of a faraway church bell marking the hour. Here and there in the distance, nestling into the sides of the hills, white villas were picked out by the sun. He intended that one of them would soon be his.

Giancarlo lifted a pair of small binoculars and adjusted the focus until it brought 'his' villa into clear view. During the many months he had been searching on the internet, he had clicked back again and again to this house. Everything about it fitted what he most desired. There were other villas and farms dotted about, but they were not close by, which suited him perfectly. He did not wish to live in an isolated place, but neither did he feel the need of neighbours. When he wanted company, there was plenty of action to be had in the gaudy seaside resort 30 minutes drive away.

The building was spacious, but not so ostentatious as to attract too much attention, something he thought he should avoid for the first couple of years at least. He could easily envisage sitting on the patio, a glass of chilled wine in his hand, looking beyond his swimming pool to the distant shimmering sea. It was expensive, of course, but Giancarlo felt he owed it to himself, that he had earned it after all the years of being under the thumb, the months of careful planning.

The first time he had visited the property a few days earlier, it had delighted him. Naturally, he had contained his delight in front of the estate agent, pointing out small defects as though they were significant, and sighing in a disappointed manner when entering a room or examining a feature. Sensing some interest, the agent revealed that the house had been on the market for several months, a fact that Giancarlo was aware of from his internet searches, and that the owners might be prepared to negotiate a little on the price for a quick sale. Giancarlo had merely shrugged and said he had several more properties to view over the coming days, and would bear that information in mind.

Two hours ago he had returned for a second viewing, and during the protracted discussions that ensued, Giancarlo let slip that this was the front-runner of two villas that interested him but, unfortunately, it was the more expensive. They embarked on the familiar elaborate dance between those with something to sell and those with a desire to buy: Giancarlo offered a sum that the agent felt sure would be rejected, but of course he would try his best. He made the phone call there and then, and swiftly confirmed that, alas, the owners were not interested in selling at that price.

These opening salvos having been completed in the time-honoured fashion, the two men moved outside and sat on the terrace with the glorious views, both of them understanding that Massio Maggiore wanted the house above all others, but would in no circumstances pay anything like the asking price. Their conversation ranged far and wide, but their thoughts never strayed from the real heart of the negotiation.

Eventually, they came to an arrangement, a somewhat private arrangement. Señor Maggiore named his final offer price for the property. He also identified a cash sum for the agent, in return for which he expected a swift acceptance by the owners, followed by a speedy legal transaction. The agent was certain he could achieve the former by use of his powers of persuasion, and the latter would be no problem since his cousin's nephew was a solicitor who specialised in conveyancing. They shook hands.

And so it was that, as he put down the binoculars, his phone rang with the news that the agent had succeeded in persuading the owners to accept Señor Maggiore's offer. He sighed with satisfaction, paid the bill, and drove in his rented car to the agent's cousin's nephew's office. There, in the presence of the agent and the solicitor, Giancarlo took out a fountain pen (a Montblanc, noted with approval by the other two men), signed the relevant forms and handed over the cash deposit for the house. The solicitor pointed out that the deposit was non-refundable, but the Señor was not troubled by this. The solicitor confirmed that the transaction would be concluded with the utmost speed, and enquired as to how the balance of the money would be paid.

"I prefer always to deal in cash," replied the Señor. "It keeps things simple." *I will sell the little Nativity*, he thought; *that should cover the house, and more besides.*

The Señor reached into his pocket and handed a thick envelope to the agent. The agent felt its thickness, but out of fastidiousness he did not immediately open it. The three men shook hands, smiling broadly.

37

Chapter 14

Using the majority of fingerprints in the husband's dressing room and the majority in the wife's dressing room, they were 99% certain that the most recent fingerprints belonged mainly to the Contessa and her husband. Of course, they would only be 100% sure when they had taken fresh prints directly from them both.

A worrying number of prints belonging to a single person were not immediately identifiable, but when Sergeant Sylvia sent the technician down to the village, it quickly became apparent that the single person was Josefina's husband. The Sergeant was struck by the number of surfaces that stupid man had managed to touch in such a short time, and she was glad she had refused to let them back into the palazzo while her investigations were carried out.

She assembled a team to look in every corner of the house, the main rooms used by the family, the staff areas, the attics and cellars, but there was no sign of the Contessa or her husband. They then spread out into the grounds, Sergeant Sylvia keeping the hapless Paulo with her as he was the only one with any knowledge of the house or its inhabitants. Between them, the team looked inside the greenhouses and garden sheds, the garage block, the outhouses, toolsheds, under each tree and behind every hedge. Nothing.

Paulo couldn't hide his relief; if they had come across a body, he would have been in even deeper trouble than he was now. "What will you do now, Sergeant?"

Though determined not to show it, especially in front of her male colleagues, Sergeant Sylvia was also relieved they had found no bodies. She had never liked the sight and smell of violent death, finding it hard to shake them from her memory afterwards.

"I will speak to the Inspector," she replied, and moved to the terrace, pulling out her mobile phone and sitting on a decorative wrought-iron chair. While waiting to be put through, her gaze ranged over the garden, taking in the small fountain, the flowers and shrubs, the lily pond. *What a beautiful place*, she thought. *If I lived here I would never want to leave it; never do anything to jeopardise it.* Clearly the Contessa and her husband had their marital troubles; what couple didn't have those? But surely they could find some way of accommodating each other, so that they could continue sharing all this?

When the Inspector came on the line, she quickly outlined the facts and he listened carefully. He had a reputation as a thorough professional, one of the few officers promoted through the ranks because of his ability, rather than a time-server elevated through patronage. He would ask the right questions, and she would respect his decisions.

"Thank you for that clear report, Sergeant. Now tell me, what is your opinion of the situation? Take your time."

"Well, Sir. From the shambolic state of the rooms and the fact that many very valuable items are missing, there has clearly been a robbery. However, the house was locked, and there is no sign of a break-in. Therefore, the robber had keys. This, and the fact that all the fingerprints belong to the Contessa, her husband and their staff, would indicate that one or more of them carried out the robbery. The Contessa was interviewed by a police officer who saw the marks of a beating on her face, and reported that she looked frightened. She confirmed that her husband had threatened her with further violence if she called the police. The Contessa's car is here, but the husband's car is not. All of this would suggest the possibility that the husband returned after our officer had left, and attacked her again." She paused.

"Please go on."

"There is no sign of a body, Sir; no trace of blood. The Contessa is missing, but we cannot find her handbag, which could mean it is still with her. Also, she has only been missing for two days, and the staff confirm that both husband and wife are frequently away, either together or at different times, often without warning. As there is no clear evidence of foul play beyond the robbery, it is entirely possible that there is a simple explanation for the Contessa's absence: that she was shaken by the original assault, called a cab and went somewhere she felt safe to recover. We have a robbery, and two missing persons, but it is not certain what the connection is between those two facts."

"Thank you again, Sergeant. I agree with your assessment. It is too soon to officially declare the Contessa a missing person, or her husband a wanted person. I suggest you continue your investigations, but keep it low key for the moment. Contact the local cab companies to see if any of them were called to the house. See if that Ferrari can be traced. And as a precaution, check with the airports and ports to see if either the Contessa or her husband has left the country. Keep me informed of progress."

"Yes, Sir." She liked the way he had said: "I suggest". It was an order, of course, but typical of him to offer this little courtesy to his juniors. She called the team onto the terrace, and gave them their instructions.

Chapter 15

Two flights and four time zones later the Contessa, tired and disorientated, finally landed in the southern hemisphere and stepped into a taxi. She had booked a small suite in a large hotel overlooking the spectacular bay set out below her. Though she had seen its picture many times, the reality was much, much better.

Her first week or so was spent recuperating from all the physical and emotional exertions she had recently undergone. She ate and slept well, swam in the hotel's pool every day, and was regularly massaged, the gorgeous young masseur commenting on the tension in her neck and shoulders. On a whim, she had her dark hair cut and coloured a honey blonde; she had manicures and pedicures, and no-one commented on the marks lingering about her face. This was, after all, a place where cosmetic surgery was available to anyone on the health service; they were all at it.

Venturing outside the hotel, she opened a bank account, and treated herself to a few shopping expeditions. Having arrived with only one suitcase, she needed a completely new wardrobe to set off the jewellery she had brought with her. After these little trips, she sat beside the hotel's swimming pool, sipping a cool drink, leafing through the Italian papers that the hotel ordered for her, and gradually acclimatising her skin to the hot sun.

A small smile played about her lips as she contemplated what would be happening back at home. That poor young policeman had clearly taken the bait, the house would be thick with police officers who would suspect the worst and, hopefully, be searching for her wicked husband. They would surely catch up with him eventually, and accuse him of kidnapping his wife, possibly even murdering her. Serve him right. What she wouldn't give to eavesdrop on that particular interview.

Meanwhile, she lay back, sun-warmed and relaxed, reflecting on the strange twists and turns of life. *Who would have thought that buying my Bugatti all those years ago would lead me half-way round the world to Rio?* Her senses were almost overwhelmed by the fragrant blossoms from the gardens, and the soft ever-present music wafting up from the beach. How lovely and sunny these Brazilians were, always singing, always smiling; so unlike the dour northern Italians. They refused to be downhearted and took life as it came. She found it very appealing.

Chapter 16

Once the team had taken all the evidence that could be retrieved, Sergeant Sylvia called Josefina to the house and told her she could resume her duties. The Sergeant made it clear that Josefina was to ring her immediately if the Contessa or her husband made contact by any means whatsoever, be it in person, by phone, or via a third person. She then asked whether the staff were still being paid. Josefina sniffed. She did not care for this Sergeant Sylvia person; she was as abrupt and bossy as the Contessa. However, she confirmed that, so far, their wages continued to be paid.

"Contact me if the situation changes in any way."

"Officer Paulo ..."

"You are to speak directly to me about anything concerning this house or its owners. I will liaise with Officer Paulo as necessary. Is that understood?"

Josefina sniffed once more, and reached for her cleaning things.

A few days later, Sergeant Sylvia reported to the Inspector that her investigations had drawn a blank: none of the local taxi companies had been called to the house on the night of the robbery; the Ferrari had not been traced, and neither the Contessa nor her husband had left the country by air or by sea.

"Of course, they could have left by road or rail, Sir. Or they could still be in Italy."

"What is the situation at the house, Sergeant?"

"The team has finished their work, and I have allowed the staff back to tidy up and continue their duties. The housekeeper has strict instructions to notify me personally should any of the staff hear from the Contessa or her husband. Meanwhile, I have directed my local officer to look in on the house every couple of days."

"Very good. Sooner or later the husband will try to sell some of the things he stole, so I have alerted relevant colleagues to keep an eye out for him. Presumably, the staff are being paid from a bank account that has a finite amount in it. Let's see whether the Contessa turns up before the funds run out."

Chapter 17

Giancarlo sank back into the plush upholstered armchair and thought back over the last few weeks.

Surprisingly, the solicitor had been as good as his word and, just a fortnight after handing over the deposit, Giancarlo returned to the south to sign the final document. It was gravely pointed out to the Señor Maggiore that this was a legal contract to purchase a property, and that once he had signed it, he would be committed to paying the balance of the price by the date specified in the contract. He nodded his understanding.

He was again asked how he intended to pay, and reiterated that he always worked in cash. The solicitor and the agent exchanged knowing glances as the Señor once more took out his exquisite pen, leaned forward and scrawled illegibly against the places marked with a cross. It was agreed that the Señor would return on the due date with the balance of the money. Following a discreet cough by the agent, the Señor confirmed that, of course, he had not forgotten their little private arrangement, which he would settle upon being handed the deeds of the house.

A few days later, the Señor hired a private room in a good hotel in Barcelona, instructing that it was to be furnished with an easel and a bottle of fine deep red wine. The dealer betrayed no reactions when he first set eyes on the little Nativity resting on the easel, but his eyes flicked back to it repeatedly as he and the Señor sat and sipped their wine, exchanging the usual pleasantries. As had been agreed in their earlier conversations, there was to be no record of this meeting and, should a satisfactory outcome be reached, the transaction would be carried out in cash and without paperwork.

45

The formalities now over, the Señor invited the dealer to examine the painting, and pretended to look out of the window as the man studied the picture from every angle, using an eye piece to peer closely at the brushwork and the frame, walking behind the easel to study the back. With permission from the Señor, the dealer lifted the painting from the easel and held it up to his eyes, tilting it this way and that, before returning it to the easel.

The Señor moved to the table to refill their glasses. Lifting the bottle, he said: "It is a fine specimen, is it not?"

"Of its type – very," replied the dealer. He was meticulously turned out, a dapper man with a pencil moustache. A tiny smile of anticipation played about his moist lips.

"How much do you value it at?"

The dealer gave a mirthless laugh: "How much are you expecting, Señor? Tens of thousands? Hundreds of thousands? Perhaps even millions?"

The Señor inclined his head modestly and waited.

"It's worthless!" the man almost spat. "You'd be lucky to get 100 euros for it on the high street."

"100 euros?" repeated Giancarlo, confused.

"It's a reproduction," the dealer went on. "An expert rendition, I'll grant you, but a reproduction nonetheless."

The dealer rambled on, but the only word Giancarlo heard was 'reproduction' – the little Nativity was a reproduction.

His mind refused to take it in, and he didn't hear the dealer leave the room.

By the next morning, Giancarlo had recovered his wits. There were several possibilities that could explain the disaster: the dealer could have been lying in order to buy a genuine masterpiece at a pittance; the little Nativity could perhaps be a reproduction, but he had many other items to sell. He would try again.

The solid silver candlesticks turned out not to be of solid silver, but he was offered a considerable sum for one of the ornate clocks, which he took with alacrity. Once more he booked the private room and arranged for a dealer, a different dealer, to look at the little Nativity as well as two other paintings. The result was the same: they were all fake.

Chapter 18

As instructed, Officer Paulo made regular trips to the palazzo. Everything seemed as it should, the gardeners busying themselves about the grounds, the sound of hammering coming from a workshop, a young cleaner bustling around the house, and Josefina barking orders to all and sundry. It was all perfectly normal, as if nothing had happened, there had been no burglary, and the master and mistress of the house had not disappeared without trace a few weeks before.

Josefina confirmed that, yes, all the staff were being paid as usual, and no, she had not heard from either of her employers, and of course, she would contact him immediately if anything changed. The more often Paulo went to the house, the more Josefina spoke to him as if he were her son, a difficult, idle son who kept getting in the way. He was certain she would have shown considerably more respect to Sergeant Sylvia.

After each visit he reported to the Sergeant. She, in turn, kept the Inspector informed on a weekly basis. The Inspector revealed that he had obtained access to the bank accounts of the Contessa and her husband. The husband's account had steadily increased over several months but been cleaned out just before the robbery; the Contessa's account had not been touched since she disappeared, except for the regular payments that went automatically into their joint account. This joint account appeared to be used to pay for household expenses such as staff wages, repairs, car maintenance, etc.

It was the Inspector's view that, sooner or later, someone would access one of the accounts, which he would continue to monitor. The Sergeant was to maintain her watch on the house. Sergeant Sylvia was honoured to be taken into the Inspector's confidence like this. Naturally, she did not pass on any of this information to young Paulo.

Exactly a month after the Contessa had last been seen, the Inspector publicly declared her a missing person, adding that her husband was being sought in connection with a robbery at their house.

The local press swarmed round the story like wasps to a pot of jam. They interviewed the Inspector, *I can only repeat my official statement*, and Sergeant Sylvia, *I have nothing further to add to the Inspector's statement.* Officer Paulo was, as instructed by his superiors, regretfully unable to comment. They interviewed Josefina and Giuseppe, the latter having a great deal to say for himself, much of it wildly unrealistic even to the journalists hungry for a juicy story. They spoke to the rest of the staff, as well as to anybody in the village who had ever glimpsed the powder blue Lamborghini or the glistening red Ferrari.

Before long the story was picked up by the nationals, who proceeded to join the dots in order to give it more impact, so that it became a classic tale of wealth and aristocracy, love and jealousy, robbery and murder. They decided that the husband had been discovered by the wife in the very act of stealing her treasures and, to stop her raising the alarm, had kidnapped her and later murdered her.

Newspapers printed pictures of husband and wife, although they were somewhat old and grainy since there didn't appear to be any more recent photographs. Reporters in helicopters salivated over the house and the gardens, lingered over the Lamborghini, but had to make do with stock shots of Ferraris. Editors in the national media waited eagerly for a body to be found, without which the story could not run for more than a day or so, and would have to be replaced with something more dramatic. Foreign media noted the event merely as a footnote; it could be elevated to a half-page once the body was found.

Chapter 19

In their early years together, Aurelia had told him many tales about her first husband. How he liked to drink and gamble, the string of mistresses, the fact that his distant relatives had given up on him years before she met him. Was it possible that the old Conte had sold many of the family treasures to fund his lifestyle? If so, he would more than likely have replaced them with reproductions in order to maintain the fiction that the aristocratic home was stuffed full of works of art. Aurelia had always believed that they were masterpieces. Indeed, she made it clear that this was one of the many things that had attracted her to the Conte. Ten years ago they had been lucky to choose a genuine painting to sell, but which of the others were copies he didn't know. He had to find out; the purchase of his villa, his entire new life, depended on it.

It was more than likely that Barcelona art dealers, though habitually obsessively secretive, did share a good laugh among themselves whenever they came across someone trying to sell a fake. Whether he was a poor, deluded sap who thought he had the real thing, or a thief who'd stolen the wrong picture, the dealers collectively sniggered at their stupidity, and individually hoped that one of their rivals had been taken in by it. He needed to try somewhere different.

Giancarlo made some phone calls, hired a car and drove the remaining paintings back over the French border, heading east. The dealers in Marseilles were as sniffy as the dealers in Barcelona, and told the same story: they were all reproductions, superb reproductions, very difficult to spot unless, of course, one was an expert.

Back in Barcelona with his useless paintings, Giancarlo contemplated what there was left to sell. He felt certain that the two remaining clocks would yield good money; the rest, well there was only one way to find out. While overjoyed to learn that the crystal ware was indeed valuable, the ceramics, which had always been carefully locked in a glass display case and only brought out on the rarest of occasions, were worthless.

He paced about the rented apartment and calculated how much he could get if he sold everything. It was a sizeable amount, but not nearly enough to cover the purchase of his beloved villa, especially when the private 'arrangements' for the agent and the solicitor were added. He thought and thought, re-doing the calculations, but nothing altered the fact that he could not afford to buy the lovely white house in the hills with its glorious view down to the sea. The time had passed very quickly since he had signed the legal, irrevocable document, and there were only two days to go to the deadline, and no way to make up the shortfall.

Giancarlo sighed with resignation. It had to be faced. He would walk away from the deal, move somewhere new, sell whatever he could, and start a new life. He would go south where the weather was hot and he could see the Mediterranean every day, but further west this time, well away from the estate agent and his cousin's nephew. He was relieved he'd had the foresight to use a hired car each time he'd met them. There was no way they could trace him; he had to keep it that way. A plan began to form: he would alter his appearance, invent a new background, and try his luck among the razzmatazz in the garish seaside towns.

Once again donning the workman's overalls, he struggled with moving everything back down to his car. He cursed the reproduction paintings in their heavy, cumbersome frames, but he didn't want to leave any trace behind of who he was, or who he might have been. Besides, he might even persuade some gullible person that the paintings were originals. Checking round the apartment, he put his hand in his pocket and it closed over his mobile phone. On a whim, he decided to make one last call before destroying it, satisfy something that had been niggling at the back of his mind. When the Marseilles dealer answered, he was surprised when the Señor asked him how old the reproductions were.

"Well, they were made at different times," he responded. "Probably by different people."

"Could you be a little more specific?"

"If you had to press me, I should estimate that they were all produced within the last ten years."

Chapter 20

Sitting outside one of the many delightful cafes along the Rio beachfront, the Contessa sipped her coffee and gazed at the sparkling blue ocean. She could never get enough of that view. Perhaps it stemmed from having spent decades in the countryside, or maybe it was because her earliest memories were of being by the water. She gazed entranced at the lithe teenagers frolicking on the sand and the little children paddling at the water's edge. Everyone looked beautiful and happy. Indeed, she too felt that way. Her face was recovering fast, and her new blonde hair set off her light tan. She had always had good legs, and her body was being honed by her daily swims in the pool. Strolling to the café that lunchtime, she was aware of admiring glances and wolf-whistles; for a woman of a certain age, it was all most gratifying.

Idly, Aurelia leafed through the Italian papers she'd brought with her from the hotel. All the usual doom and gloom, of course; well, she wasn't at all interested in any of that. She heard a woman's scream nearby and looked up, but it was just one of the near-naked girls being chased by a near-naked boy with a water pistol. The beaches were always thronging with life and laughter, as if nobody ever did any work. Looking back to the paper, she turned a few pages, then suddenly sat bolt upright. Right in front of her was her own photograph, and Giancarlo's. And there was her house, and her car. She read the article swiftly, read it again more slowly, and sank back into the chair.

So, it had happened at last. She had been expecting it, of course, even desiring it. But at that moment her mind had been so far away that the article had come as a shock. She scrutinised her photograph carefully. It was of poor quality and neither recent nor particularly flattering. *I look quite different now*, she thought. It wasn't only her physical appearance in the picture, but the tetchy expression on her face. Aurelia hadn't been tetchy since first waking up in Rio.

The waiter appeared to offer her more coffee. Instinctively she moved to cover the paper, but then remembered that he would speak Portuguese, and probably couldn't read Italian. She smiled broadly at him, saying yes, she would love another coffee. As he reached to remove her cup, he glanced at the newspaper on the table, but there was no hint of recognition in his eyes as he returned her smile.

Aurelia relaxed. She read the article once more, enjoying the description of herself as "a beautiful, rather haughty Contessa" who lived in a "palazzo", savouring the implication, almost an assertion, that her wicked, scheming husband had robbed and murdered her. She wanted to laugh out loud. Well, Giancarlo was wicked and scheming, and who knows what else he was capable of. *I wonder if he's seen this article?* she thought. *I do hope so.* She almost squirmed with pleasure at the fear and panic he would experience at the thought of being pursued by the police for her murder. He knew he hadn't murdered her, of course, but he could hardly go to the police and admit to the robbery, but say she had been very much alive when he'd last seen her. Supposing they didn't believe him – why would they? Everything pointed to the opposite. No, he would slink into a corner somewhere and hide for as long as possible.

And so what if she were to be recognised here in Rio, and her existence reported to the police? Simple. She would explain that it had all been a terrible mistake: she and her husband had had a fierce row triggered by the robbery; he had a violent temper, and she had felt shaken and disorientated by the argument, and decided to get right away; she hadn't contacted Giancarlo because she wanted to teach him a lesson, but had no idea that anyone thought she was actually missing, or even dead. That possibility had never crossed her mind. She would apologise profusely for all the fuss that had been caused by this silly misunderstanding.

Aurelia looked back towards the sea and smiled. Inclining her head, she gazed at the apartment blocks that ringed the wide bay. *I wonder what it would be like to live here?*

Chapter 21

It had been a long, frustrating afternoon waiting for the Señor Maggiore to arrive. He was due at 2 p.m., but 4 o'clock passed and still he had not appeared. Several times they tried ringing him, only to find that his phone was switched off. Sitting in the solicitor's office, the agent peered disdainfully at the walls covered in grandiose certificates and photographs of a beaming solicitor in the company of several dignitaries and celebrities. He had been a boastful boy, and had not grown out of the habit.

On the desk in front of them lay the paperwork and the keys to the villa. The agent and the solicitor persuaded themselves that he had obviously been unavoidably delayed, was unable to contact them, and would appear at any minute. They chatted on and off about family matters, local politics, sport. Their eyes frequently strayed to the glass door, expecting soon to see the smartly-dressed Señor with the perfect swept-back salt-and-pepper hair, typical of a stylish Italian businessman. When they ran out of conversation, each man quietly contemplated how he planned to spend the extra commission he would gain for rushing the purchase through so speedily and, it had to be said, somewhat illegally. They had agreed early on that they would not tell their wives about this considerable bonus.

By 7 p.m. the agent and the solicitor acknowledged that the Señor would not be coming during office hours, and they left for dinner with their respective families. In theory, they had until midnight to close the deal. It was just possible that the Señor would contact them during the evening, and they could head back to the office for the handover. They met up in a bar at 11 p.m., speculating as to what could have delayed the Señor, and agreeing that they would not show their displeasure at his tardiness and discourtesy until the formalities were complete and he had handed over a bulky envelope to each of them.

They were startled when the young solicitor's mobile phone rang, but it was only his wife asking when he would be home. Embarrassed to be perceived as under the marital thumb, he quickly ended the call. The agent wondered aloud what they would do if the Señor did not turn up at all, but they dismissed this notion as ridiculous. After all, he had paid over a sizeable deposit on the villa, a sum that most people would not want to forfeit. They knew little of his financial circumstances. Very distinguished to look at, he could almost have been an aristocrat, but the fact that he used hire cars and always paid cash indicated that he might not be a saint. This didn't bother them in the least. Everyone had to duck and dive a little to make a reasonable living.

At midnight, they began to consider their options. A few weeks before when the Señor had insisted on a swift purchase, the solicitor had advised his uncle's cousin that it was not possible to speed up the process because the Señor was a foreign national, and did not have all the required documents. And they had made a bold decision: they would buy the villa themselves, and then sell it on to the Señor. He would know nothing of this arrangement.

Having watched him sign papers he had barely read, they believed he took the traditional Italian view of official documents. Also, while his spoken Spanish was quite adequate, perhaps he did not read Spanish so well. Either way, he had signed whatever was put in front of him without realising he was buying the villa not from the current owner, but from them. Legally, the villa would not actually be his property for several more weeks, but that was a mere detail. The owner would have his money, the agent and the solicitor would have their bonuses, the Señor would have his house – everyone would be happy.

The owner had been keen to sell, but had hesitated when he realised the purchasers were the local agent and solicitor. Why would they do that unless they already had a buyer and were going to sell it on at a profit? In which case, why shouldn't the owner have that profit himself? He attempted to raise the price. They threatened to pull out. Finally, it was agreed that while the price would remain the same, the deposit would be greater and would be paid in cash, and the penalties for late payment of the balance would be increased.

The agent and the solicitor had had to spend some of the Señor's cash to encourage the bureaucracy along, and were disappointed that the rest had to go towards the deposit. But this still fell far short of the new arrangement, and they were obliged to raise the remainder by pooling all their savings, and by using money they were holding in trust on behalf of their other clients. The Señor's final payment would settle all these debts, but of the Señor there was no trace, and now they were in deep trouble.

Chapter 22

The Contessa had come to a satisfactory agreement with the estate agent, a rather good-looking young man – but then, weren't they all good-looking around here? It was agreed that she would rent the apartment for 3 months, with a view to buying it if she found it to her liking. She found it to her liking the first time she stepped inside: light, airy rooms, elegantly furnished, a long balcony adorned with tubs of flowering plants and swing chairs, and spectacular views across the wide bay. She would have bought it on the spot, except that she needed to make a few financial arrangements first.

Aurelia had had no long-term plan when she set out from her house on that dreadful night her husband had robbed her. Her only thought had been to cause Giancarlo as much trouble as possible, and to get away for a while. It had been a surprise, and a delight, to find herself falling in love with Rio. Rio made her feel young; it utterly beguiled her: the climate, the beautiful people, the ever-present music, a sense that the main purpose of everyone's life was to have fun. But if she intended to live here for a while, she would have to attend to her finances.

First, there was the matter of raising enough cash to buy the apartment. The solution was quite simple: she would sell one of the old Conte's family treasures. One by one as she had received the reproductions, the Contessa had taken the precaution of setting aside a small number of originals to give her future flexibility. She had most of the authentic pieces locked away under the scrupulous care of the Swiss, who showed no surprise at the number or value of the items. For them, it was routine; something people did in order to reduce their insurance premiums to a sane level. But she kept a handful of valuables back, each of them separately and securely stored in a different location, with herself as the only key-holder.

Now, she sat on her balcony with a glass of chilled wine and thought about which treasure she could most easily part with. This was a difficult decision as she hated to lose any of them. Indeed, she had almost come to believe that the collection had been in *her* family for generations, rather than in the old Conte's family. But needs must. There was a dark and rather depressing painting featuring John the Baptist's head on a plate. She could live without that in her life. The Contessa picked up the phone and pressed the buttons. It rang and rang while she sipped her wine, until she heard a grunt at the other end and pictured the lank, greasy hair, the strange eyes, each a different colour and set unevenly in the face.

"Luigi. It's me."

It took him a while to focus. More than likely he was high. The only member of her extended family to be born without the advantages of good looks, cousin Luigi had proved useful on many occasions. In exchange for keeping him well funded, she could rely on him to carry out her requests discreetly. Long ago he had agreed never to divulge her new name or whereabouts to the rest of the clan, on condition that she did the same for him. He knew how much her title and status meant to her, and how compromised she would be if her high-minded circle found out about her background. She knew that he had 'borrowed' from just about every felon in their neighbourhood, failing to refund any of it, a rather foolish oversight given the habitual violence meted out in those streets. The need for secrecy was mutual.

"Hey, cuz," he boomed. "How's it hanging?"

Aurelia closed her eyes. Even though well into his 40s, Luigi persisted in talking as though he were a young black rapper from the projects.

"I need you to do a little job for me," she said.

"Well why else would you be ringing?" he laughed.

"I want you to take something to the Dottore."

"Jus' like before, eh cuz?

"Yes, just like before. I will send you a key. Ring me when you get it and I will give you the password, and tell you when to take the item to the Dottore."

"Right."

She sighed. "Is that clear, Luigi? I want you to repeat it to me, word for word."

He did so, using a funny voice and giggling at his own hilarity. But he got the instructions right. She could always rely on him clearing the fog when he had to. She trusted him – well, he was family. But her trust did not extend to letting him know where the other pieces were stored, and she changed the password every time. It was not wise to tell someone like Luigi, who loved his drugs, too much about her business at any one moment. He had never let her down before, but still, she would take no chances.

Chapter 23

The blocks of high-rise hotels and apartments were nowhere near as beautiful as his stunning white villa with its sweeping views down to the sea, but they did have one major advantage: anonymity. After getting the lie of the land, Giancarlo leased an apartment in what seemed to be a fashionable quarter. He also rented a lock-up to hold the paintings and other treasures.

It was regrettable that he had had to forfeit the deposit paid out on the villa. It irked him to think of that slimy agent and the pompous solicitor smirking over pocketing so much of his cash. He hoped they had been through all kinds of grief when they realised he wouldn't be turning up and they would be unable to get their grubby hands on any more of his money. Well, they had nothing to complain about: for very little effort they had received a sizeable reward, and he would not waste another moment thinking about them. His focus would be on his future.

He cultivated a little goatee beard, and had his greying hair dyed a rich brown. While waiting for his own hair to grow, he bought a length of false hair and fixed it to the back of his head in a samurai knot, a look he had observed on some of the young men playing football on the sand. He ran along the beach every day, becoming fitter and more toned. He strolled the length of the promenade and round to the marina, taking note of the kinds of clothes young men wore. And when the transformation was complete, he looked in the mirror and saw a much younger man, good-looking, stylish, with just a little touch of the bohemian.

In the evenings, he sat in bars and restaurants, and watched. All the time, watching the women – young and

not-so-young: where did the wealthiest hang out? how
could he get to meet them?   What he sought was tourists,
tourists with money, women who would stay at the resort
for a few days or a few weeks; women who were looking
for fun with no strings; women who would be grateful for
feeling young and attractive again. *Giancarlo, once more
you are a gigolo*, and he laughed. He had no intention of
repeating the mistake he had made in letting Aurelia
control his life. No, he would be the master of his own
destiny. Not for him a marriage, or even a long-term
affair, no matter how wealthy the woman.

It was the first time he had thought about Aurelia for
weeks. He wondered whether she would try to find him,
perhaps hire a private detective. She had a vindictive
streak, and though she wouldn't want him back after such
a betrayal, she was quite capable of trying to track him
down and have him hurt.

Well, when it came to betrayals, what about hers? For
years she had been secretly selling off heirlooms and
replacing them with fakes.   That would have taken
considerable effort, and why go to all that trouble, if not to
rob him of his share of the family wealth. For all he knew
she might even have been planning to replace him with
another man; perhaps that was also the reason for the
recent facelift.   Such a cunning woman.   He had
underestimated her. For his own protection, it would be
wise to be a little bit more mysterious in his dealings with
strangers.

"Pardon me."

Giancarlo almost jumped at the interruption, looking up to
see two ladies, arm-in-arm, beaming down at him.

"Oh dear, we didn't mean to startle you, did we, Ella
Mae?"

"No," Ella Mae giggled. "It's just that you looked as if you carried the troubles of the world on your shoulders, and we thought you might need a little company."

Americans, early 50s, covered in jewels, and just a bit tipsy. They were perfect.

Chapter 24

Like all her siblings, the Contessa had learnt with her mother's milk how to spot people who, while not actual crooks, were open to bending the rules. And she was practised in the various incentives that might be needed to tip any waverers over the line. With the Dottore it had been ridiculously easy. She had sniffed out his secret early on: he was not, in fact, a Dottore. But she recognised that he valued his title just as much as she valued hers. It was intrinsic to his business, the art world being littered with academic and aristocratic nomenclature. Once he knew that she knew he was not a Dottore, he began to blink a lot more frequently and straightened a bow tie that was already rigidly horizontal. So she had mentioned a small commission that she had in mind, and named a sum that would be his if he would but take the commission, and they were up and running in no time.

He operated as a legitimate art dealer, but his main income came from clients who regarded buying or selling on the open market as an invitation either to tax inspectors, or to their business rivals or, in a few cases, to their impoverished electorate, all of whom wished to poke their noses into affairs that were none of their concern. He had already sold two of her pieces, and soon he would be salivating over the John the Baptist. From previous experience, it would not take him long to transfer a huge sum, minus his fee, into her account on the small Caribbean island. Thus, she would buy the Rio apartment with cash, and have enough left over to live in conspicuous comfort for some considerable time.

Keeping her beloved Italian palazzo going was more complicated. The not-so-beloved Josefina needed to be paid every month, as did the other staff. Such an old and venerable house also required frequent maintenance. The whole venture positively consumed money, which was routinely paid out of the joint bank account she held with Giancarlo. When last she looked, this account had a reasonably good balance in it. But it would need to be topped up before too long.

The Contessa briefly toyed with the idea of getting rid of the complication by getting rid of the house, but even the act of considering it made her realise how much it meant to her. She loved the house and the grounds. Besides, owning a palazzo, no matter how modest, was central to her image as a member of the nobility.

Of course, she herself had merely married into the aristocracy, having been born in a slum. By the time she met the old Conte she had fabricated a more interesting past, and now the Conte was long dead. Giancarlo had his suspicions, but had never managed to worm much out of her, and right now he was nowhere to be found. Who was there left to know about her shabby origins? She would keep her palazzo. It might be fun to spend the Brazilian summers in Rio and the Italian summers in Italy. Her life would be lived in perpetual sunshine.

The complication arose from topping-up the joint account. Aurelia would have plenty of money once the John the Baptist was sold, but she realised that movement on any of her Italian accounts would soon attract the attention of anyone snooping around. Newspaper reports had described her and Giancarlo as missing, and had failed to disguise their desire for a body to be found. This meant that the police would surely have trawled through their bank statements in an attempt to figure out what had happened. Paying in the money directly would identify her whereabouts immediately. She had a lawyer with a highly flexible attitude to the law, and could transfer funds to him to be paid into the household account. She had long ago bought his loyalty, and though this would be enough for him to delay any official investigations, he would not deliberately conceal the money's origins if directly confronted by police undertaking a potential murder enquiry.

The Contessa found it amusing to be 'missing'. She would like to remain missing for a while longer. There had to be some other way to keep her palazzo going.

Chapter 25

The agent and the solicitor had to admit that they were worried, though neither would confess the fear they both felt in the pit of their stomachs; that would be too unmanly. Provided there were no unforeseen bills, they could conceal from their wives the empty savings accounts. Far more urgent was the absence of their clients' deposits for their new homes. People were always pushing to speed up conveyancing, and they could only hide behind 'unavoidable bureaucratic delays' for so long. The Señor had to be found, and quickly.

Though he had never given them a permanent address and did not own a car, they had been careful to note the name of the car hire company he used, and the various cars' registration numbers.

From time to time the solicitor had occasion to use a firm of private investigators. Solicitors had many errant clients, whose associates were equally questionable. He was accustomed to being lied to, and for people to disappear without warning, or to appear when they should not. In such circumstances, a private investigator could often sort out the problem for the benefit of the solicitor.

He called the managing director and explained that one of his more important clients needed to find a middle-aged Italian man who tended to operate below the radar. He described the man's physical appearance, spelt out the name he used, and details of the car hire. The matter was urgent, and needed to be handled by someone who was very discreet.

"I have just the agent," said the investigator.

They agreed terms. Then there was nothing for the estate agent and the solicitor to do but wait for news, and to drum up new business as fast as possible to begin replenishing their empty coffers.

Chapter 26

The Caribbean was gorgeous any time of year except, of course, during the height of the hurricane season. But Aurelia wasn't there for a holiday. After freshening up at her hotel, she went straight to the bank. The young clerk afforded her every courtesy, as well he might, given the amount she had deposited in his bank.

"I wish to have a lump sum transferred to an account in Italy that I hold jointly with my husband, Giancarlo."

"Certainly, madam. I will just take the details."

He tapped into the computer, found the account she directed him to and noted the amount.

"There is just one other thing," she smiled. "I wish the money to be transferred in my husband's name. He is so thoughtful and always likes to take care of the palazzo for me. Would that be possible?"

He hesitated for a fraction.

She reached for her handbag: "I would be particularly grateful."

The clerk's strong face erupted into a huge smile, and she was temporarily blinded by two rows of dazzling white teeth. "Of course, madam."

Yes, she thought, *anything is possible here and no questions asked, provided you pay enough money.*

"Excellent. You have been most helpful."

The next day she was on a plane back to Rio.

No doubt the transaction would be traced back to her sooner or later, and she could explain it all away as a misunderstanding on the part of the bank clerk. But in the meantime the police would draw their own conclusions, and those conclusions could lead to considerable discomfort for her worthless husband. What a tantalising thought.

Chapter 27

Sergeant Sylvia was collecting her elderly mother from the church where she was attending Mass when her mobile rang. It was the Inspector.

"I am so sorry to ring you on a Sunday, Sergeant. I do hope you will forgive the intrusion."

Clearly this was not a question, but an assumption.

"It's not a problem, Sir." The church bells rang out in the background.

"I wanted to alert you to some interesting developments with regard to the owners of the palazzo di Tramonti."

She stiffened, tugging a stray strand of peroxide hair into place. Officer Paulo dropped in on the palazzo every week to question Josefina and take a look around. He reported back to her faithfully after these visits, each time saying nothing had changed. This in turn she had relayed to the Inspector. Had Paulo messed up again? She hadn't forgotten the fiasco of him allowing the household staff to roam around a crime scene. Had he failed to notice something of significance?

"Has anything happened, Sir?"

"Indeed it has, Sergeant. Or rather, I should say that two things have happened."

Oh God, Paulo has missed something important. Sylvia braced herself, although she could detect no hint of criticism in his voice. Worshippers began streaming out of the church, and she spotted her mother hovering on the steps, looking for her. She crossed the road.

"Firstly, our friends in the art world have brought to my attention the brief appearance of a certain painting whose last known owner was the Contessa di Tramonti."

Sylvia had no 'friends in the art world', but appreciated being included within the Inspector's orbit.

"Needless to say, it disappeared without trace, presumably into the black market."

Sylvia allowed herself the smallest feeling of relief. Valuable paintings and black markets had nothing to do with Officer Paulo's universe.

"Secondly, a rather large sum has been deposited in the joint account of the Contessa and her husband."

She stopped. This was the account used to pay for the maintenance of the house and the staff to run it, and the only people who would be interested in the upkeep of the palazzo were the Contessa and her husband.

"Do we know which one of them deposited the money, Sir?" she ventured.

"The funds were transferred from an account in the Caribbean in the name of Giancarlo di Tramonti."

"I see." Her mother began to shuffle towards her, left foot swathed in a furry slipper on account of her bunion. "I wonder, Sir ..." she hesitated.

"Please continue, Sergeant. I have great respect for your views in this matter."

Sylvia failed to suppress a beam, glad that the Inspector could not see it, though her mother did, and beamed back. Sylvia took her arm and guided her to the car.

"Both the sale of the painting and the bank deposit could have been arranged by one person, and it is looking increasingly like the husband, as there is still no sign of the wife. However, it strikes me as odd that a man who may have assaulted and murdered his wife would plan to reclaim the house one day. It is just possible that they are both in it together; that they are operating some sort of scam that requires their temporary disappearance. Meanwhile, they want to keep the palazzo in good order for when they return, no doubt with an interesting story to explain their absence."

"I commend you for maintaining an open mind, Sergeant. That is the hallmark of good police work. I share your caution. The fact that we have found no trace of either the Contessa or her husband means that one, or both, of them have gone to considerable lengths to cover their tracks. It would be bizarre for the husband to reveal his actions when he surely knows we will be on the look-out, or for either of them to simply waltz back into the palazzo at some future date. For the time being my focus will be on pursuing the husband to see if we can trace his whereabouts via the banks. Meanwhile, I suggest you continue your surveillance of the palazzo to see if we can't tempt someone out of the shadows."

"I need the toilet, Sylvia" came a small voice.

"Now, Sergeant, I really must let you get back to your family."

Chapter 28

Everything had been surprisingly easy. That potent mixture of impeccable charm, courteous manners, sensitive listening, a knowing sensuality – all had come back to him as simply as flicking a switch. And of course, an initial generosity appropriate to a man of means. Women, young and old, fell for him. Or at least, they fell for what he represented, for whatever was missing from their lives: love, romance, danger, desire, the heady recklessness of youth, the reassuring experience of age, simple companionship, straightforward fun.

And in return they were willing to pay. Not in a tacky sense, of course. Giancarlo did not wish to present himself as a prostitute. Rather, he was treated to lunches and dinners in classy restaurants, taken on extravagant outings, clusters of chips were handed to him in the casino. Most of the women loved going shopping, and when they discovered he was as knowledgeable about designer labels as they were, it seemed to double their retail pleasure. They indulged him with couture clothes and elegant furniture, and an almost constant succession of presents.

Naturally, he made a show of refusing all gifts, but when they were pressed upon him, well, what was a gentleman to do? He was careful to choose wealthy women, and had almost lost count of the number of watches he had received, often encrusted with diamonds. Rings, wrist chains, neck chains, all gold; cufflinks and tie pins studded with rubies, sapphires, emeralds. Even so, some of the gifts were extraordinary.

Tatiana was from Ukraine. Clearly she had once been one of those willowy, blonde ice maidens the Eastern bloc seemed to specialise in, and now she was just a little past her prime. Following the break-up of the Soviet Union her husband had made a fortune, which he thought entitled him to a string of young mistresses. Their children were fully grown, and she had sought a divorce, but he wished to remain married because it suited his carefully contrived image as a family man. So he gave her a platinum credit card, and she spent his money with alacrity. She knew that he knew she bought presents for other men, and it gave her a delicious sense of justice. "The man sins, the man must pay".

Tatiana had an enormous sense of fun, and could hold her drink like a sailor. Sometimes Giancarlo struggled to remember that she was just business, and was swept up in her zest for life. One day, Tatiana bought him a Maserati "because you are Italian", and had it delivered wrapped in a giant bow. Gazing at it, they both collapsed in laughter: he, for the sheer audacity of the gift, and she, because it was a finger to her husband. At the end of her stay, Tatiana was tucked into the Maserati, and he drove her to the airport, where they said a tearful farewell.

Giancarlo sold most of the gifts as soon as the women had departed. Once they had gone, he no more thought about them than a bee thought about the flower it had just left. He simply looked for the next flower. Most of the women understood the nature of the transaction without it ever being discussed. They seemed to regard it as a holiday fling. One or two showed signs of wanting to get more serious, but he nipped this in the bud by revealing, with appropriate solemnity, that he had a wife living in an Italian institution whom he would never abandon.

He drove to his habitual café on the marina. The owner nodded to him in recognition from inside as Giancarlo took his usual seat outside. Gazing beyond the Maserati to the flotilla of yachts, he mentally calculated the amount of money he had accumulated from these gifts. It was almost enough to embark on his new plan of buying properties. The resort appeared to have no off-season. Tourists arrived all year round, and there were plenty of people wishing to rent up-market apartments. Giancarlo had long presented himself as a businessman with interests in real estate. Why not make it a reality? He would select a couple of Aurelia's heirlooms stored in his lock-up, drive to the city, and test them on the art market. If he struck lucky with at least one of them he would start looking for suitable properties immediately.

His favourite waitress emerged with his coffee. She had a lovely face, fresh and clean without a trace of make-up. He thanked her for the coffee and she blushed slightly, as she always did whenever she served him. She looked very young.

"Permesso, Señorita. May I ask your name?"

"Mamen," she replied.

"That's an unusual name. Is it Spanish?"

"Yes, Señor. It's short for Maria Carmen."

"A charming name," he said. "I think Spanish girls must be like Italian girls in that so many of them are called Maria."

"Oh yes, all my friends are called Maria something-or-other, Maria Jose, Maria Luz. So we try to make them different by shortening them . ."

It was the longest sentence she had ever spoken to him, and she stopped abruptly as if suddenly fearing she had over-stepped the mark.

He gave her his most winning smile. "I wonder, Señorita Mamen, if your boss would mind if you sat with me for a moment to help me make a little decision? I would, of course, be delighted to buy you a coffee or something, whatever you would like."

She hesitated, glancing through the window, wanting to stay but unsure of herself.

"Please," he gestured to the chair. "Wait there while I go and ask him."

He went inside and spoke to the owner, and when he came back outside with a tall glass of coke, she was still standing by the chair. The strongest feeling swept over him. She was attractive, certainly, but it took him a moment to identify his overriding emotion: protectiveness. In that instant she seemed like the daughter he'd never had; the granddaughter, if he was being completely honest: fresh, vulnerable, unprepared for how cruel the world could be. They sat and sipped their drinks.

"Now, Señorita Mamen .."

"You can call me Mamen, if you like; everybody does."

"Very well. Mamen. Now, my problem is this. I have to go to an official function – it will be very boring, as usual," he waved his hand dismissively. "I will be wearing a light grey suit and have been advised to wear a tie, but being colour-blind I cannot decide whether to wear a blue tie or a brown tie."

"Blue," she said immediately. "You should always wear blue, because of your eyes." She stopped again and stared at the table, swallowing hard. She sipped her drink, holding the glass in both hands.

As he was driving back to his apartment, a small warning voice sounded in Giancarlo's ear: *What are you doing, Giancarlo? There is no official function, no colour-blindness. This girl is not one of your rich tourists that you have to tempt like a trout and reel in to your net. Why are you playing these games with her?* The truth was that he found her utterly enchanting and was looking for excuses to talk to her, to find a reason for meeting her without scaring her off. It was obvious that she had a small crush on him. Perhaps he could take an interest in her welfare, raise her sights from the café towards a better life? Maybe they could develop a friendship?

That evening Mamen was still playing on his mind as he pushed through the revolving doors of the hotel lobby, and walked straight into a woman in the foyer. He was profuse in his apologies as he bent to retrieve her handbag, automatically noting its Prada logo, and her bejewelled hand. She didn't look Spanish, so he spoke in the universal language of English:

"Please forgive me, madam. I am so clumsy. How can I possibly make amends? Could I perhaps offer you a drink?"

They sat at the tall stools in the hotel bar. Her name was Klaar; he thought she might be Dutch or Belgian. She was spending a few days in Spain to escape the drab northern weather. Alas, her husband could not join her due to his business commitments. He gave her his full attention: *So, Giancarlo, here we go again.*

Chapter 29

The estate agent was up in the hills at the house he and the solicitor owned but didn't want, showing it to some potential clients who didn't want it either, but who were enjoying snooping around a villa they couldn't afford. Meanwhile, his cousins's nephew was staring glumly at a bank statement when the call came through from the private detective agency.

"I believe we have found your man."

The solicitor jerked bolt upright. "Where? Please don't tell me he's gone to Australia."

"No, no. He is right here, in Spain, over to the south-west. My agent is filming him right now – I'll send it over to your computer. He looks a bit different from the description you gave me, but not so very different, and everything else we know about him fits. My agent has been very thorough, but to be sure we need your confirmation."

The solicitor scrambled to punch the keyboard, knocking over a cold cup of coffee in the process. He peered at the screen and saw a man strolling beside a marina. The filming was from a distance; palm trees and traffic occasionally obscured the subject, until the camera zoomed in for a close-up. It looked very like the Señor; perhaps a younger version of the Señor? He ambled along as though he didn't have a care in the world, gazed at the yachts bobbing gently on the water, and then bent to open the door of a Maserati. A Maserati! If the Señor could afford a car like that, he could certainly afford to pay the solicitor and his uncle's cousin what they were due.

"That's definitely him," he spluttered.

"Good. We have successfully completed our mission to locate the subject - and in remarkably good time, if I may say so. I will forward the details of his whereabouts." He paused, but when the solicitor said nothing he continued: "Do you have any further instructions, or should I send you my invoice as usual?"

The screen went blank as the private detective turned off the link.

"Keep watching him," said the solicitor. "I need to confer with my associate, but we may want you to retrieve what belongs to us." He put the phone down.

So, it's about money, thought the private detective. *It's always about money. Sometimes it's about sex, but there's usually money somewhere in the mix. Well, if cash is to be squeezed from the Italian gigolo on behalf of the self-important solicitor, then the price will be adjusted to reflect that the initial surveillance operation has now moved up a gear.*

Within hours he had been commissioned to collect what was owing to the solicitor and his associate. He rang his agent and they agreed tactics.

Chapter 30

The Inspector's office was of a generous size and furnished entirely without fuss, a reflection of the man himself. He stood up to greet Sergeant Sylvia, and motioned her to a chair. She noticed a framed photograph on his desk, taken in a summer garden: the Inspector and his elegant wife, two grown-up daughters, and the Down's son hugging an enormous floppy dog, all of them laughing as if they'd just heard the most wonderful joke.

"Thank you for sparing the time to come and see me, Sergeant."

It had been a direct order, of course, but it was these small civilities that so endeared him to her. She was almost a little bit in love with him, except that Sylvia had rarely found men to be lovable. In any event, she would risk life and limb if he asked her to.

"I have a small assignment for you, Sergeant, if you are prepared to accept it."

Sylvia almost stopped breathing. She had been tempting the gods; he was actually going to ask her to risk life and limb.

"There is no real danger involved, but I thought you might find it interesting."

"Thank you, Sir."

"But first, let me bring you up to speed on developments in the Tramonti case. As you know, we have been keeping an eye out for both the Contessa and her husband, but particularly the husband. I put the word out among colleagues in several countries, and one of them came back with information that a middle-aged Italian man had been trying to sell fake art works on the black market in Spain."

"Fake?"

"Yes, that surprised me, too. However, the other details fit our man. It could be a huge coincidence, but as we police officers don't like coincidences, it seemed worth looking into. Anyway, our Spanish colleagues very kindly agreed to pursue this lead for us, and after some excellent foot work, they believe they have tracked him down to a Mediterranean holiday resort where he appears to be living the high life. They need us to confirm that he's our man, and then say what we want them to do."

He opened a file and spread out several photographs on the desk. "Take a look at these and tell me what you think."

Sylvia leaned forward. The pictures were very clear, even the close-ups, though they must have been taken some distance from the subject. They featured a man in a variety of settings: at a restaurant table, emerging from a casino, sitting outside a cafe.

"He seems similar to the husband, from the few photographs we have of him," she ventured, "although he looks to be a little younger than I expected. But as I have never actually seen Signor di Tramonti in the flesh, I couldn't be totally sure."

"Quite. Therefore, we need to find somebody who knows the man by sight, but who won't go blabbing about it. Can you think of a suitable person?"

Was this the 'small assignment' he had in mind? It doesn't seem that onerous. Sylvia pondered. The palazzo's staff had had the most direct and recent contact with the di Tramontis, but it was obvious that Josefina had a soft spot for the husband, and her own husband was clearly a blabbermouth, so it would be unwise to involve them at this stage. There was only one other possible candidate.

"Officer Paulo would be the one to ask, Sir. He has seen the husband from time to time, although from a distance, and can be relied on to keep things to himself."

"Very good, Sergeant. If your Officer confirms that this man is indeed the husband, I wondered if you would be so kind as to go to Spain and have a little chat with him?"

Ah, so that is the assignment. Sylvia was not quite able to disguise her excitement.

"It would be an honour, Sir."

Chapter 31

The Contessa put down the phone and gazed across the bay, for the first time not really seeing it. She had been wise to slip the young bank clerk a small envelope bulging with dollars, and it hadn't taken long for him to repay her kindness.

"I thought I should alert you, Madam, to the fact that official enquiries have been made regarding the transfer you authorised when you came to our offices, the transfer in your husband's name."

"And by 'official enquiries' you mean ...?"

"The police, Madam."

"Of course, the police. And what were the police told?"

"What they are always told in these circumstances, Madam: that all our customers' transactions are strictly confidential", the young clerk sounded almost self-righteous in his affirmation of company policy.

"How much do you think they can work out for themselves?"

"They know only the date and amount of the transfer, and the name in which the money was transferred. My bank would never confirm these details, nor divulge anything further. "

"Thank you. You have been most helpful," she cooed down the line, "and if you hear of anything else, may I rely on you to let me know? I would be most grateful."

"Certainly, Madam. I will contact you immediately."

Of course you will, smiled the Contessa to herself. *You know just how grateful I can be, and there's plenty more where that came from.*

So the police will be looking for Giancarlo. And if they find him, he will have to explain not only his wife's disappearance, but also the tax haven bank account, neither of which he knows anything about.

How I would love to be a fly on the wall when that particular conversation takes place. Get out of that, Giancarlo.

Chapter 32

Klaar had proved to be good company, and was one of the many women who preferred romance to actual sex. This was often a relief for Giancarlo. In his youth he had been turned on by almost any female who was willing to play, but these days things were not quite so … reliable. The only down side with Klaar was that, despite dripping with diamonds, so far she was not very forthcoming with the sort of treats he had come to expect. After a few days, she was obliged to make a brief trip home to Belgium and the husband to sort out some "business matters", but on her return to Spain she would, he was sure, begin to bestow on him the little tokens of affection he had grown used to receiving from the women who so clearly enjoyed his attentions.

Klaar's temporary absence was like a small holiday for Giancarlo, the first real break he had managed since embarking on this new, and rather rewarding, career. He had headed straight for the café on the marina, sipping coffee in the sunshine and waiting patiently when Mamen was called away to serve other customers. He noticed that she was quite easy with others, but was self-conscious to a degree he found charming when, at his invitation, she sat with him, nursing her coke. While he chatted away, offering small pieces of information about himself in an attempt to draw her out, he saw her gaze move to his Maserati several times. Presumably she had never ridden in such a car before. Perhaps he could find a way to invite her for a drive without completely scaring her off.

As lunchtime approached, the tables began to fill. Mamen apologised that she must return to her work, and disappeared inside the cafe. Her innocence delighted him. She was so different from the women he regarded as his 'clients', some of whom were quite needy or demanding. She asked for nothing, expected nothing, but it was clear that she liked to see him.

The next day Giancarlo was disappointed to learn that Mamen wasn't there. When he enquired, the café owner gave him an old-fashioned look; it was a look that said *I've got the measure of you and your sort, and I'm not impressed.* Out loud he said that Mamen had been called home urgently and would be gone several days. Giancarlo cursed his bad luck. He had intended to suggest a little drive in his Maserati, just a short trip around the town, nothing that might alarm her.

He sat gazing at the yachts bobbing about on the sparkling sea, and sipped his coffee. Without Mamen or Klaar, he would have a few days by himself with nothing specific in mind. That hadn't happened in a long time, for he tended to plan each day meticulously. His wife would not recognise such diligence. Aurelia had always made it clear she regarded him as some sort of human jellyfish, floating aimlessly through life with no direction, merely open to whatever opportunities came along. That woman had never recognised his innate talents.

He hadn't thought about Aurelia lately, and now found himself wondering what she was up to. No doubt she was publicly flapping about her missing heirlooms and wicked husband, while secretly sniggering at her deception of Giancarlo. In fact, he wouldn't put it past her to claim on the insurance for the missing items. This thought made him sit bolt upright. Yes, that is exactly what that crafty woman would do. She would become even wealthier, while he had to work for his living. Giancarlo felt outraged. Aurelia would be laughing at everyone, but especially her husband. If only he could find a way to wipe the smirk off her face.

It didn't take him long to think of something. It was obvious, really. He would threaten to expose her little game unless, of course, he received a cut of the proceeds. He had a few days without any commitments; he would drive back to Italy and see what she was up to.

He'd had the foresight to acquire a new passport and driving licence bearing photographs showing his current appearance, but still in the name of Massio Maggiore, so he could come and go as he pleased. But it seemed prudent to leave the Maserati at the apartment; it was rather conspicuous – that was, after all, part of its attraction. Instead, he hired an anonymous family car and drove across the Spanish countryside, careful to avoid the places where he might be recognised by the estate agent or his cousin's nephew, or any of the art dealers he had approached.

The next day he was sitting in the car among the trees surrounding the palazzo, binoculars trained on the driveway, smiling at the little surprise he would give his wife.

Chapter 33

Officer Paulo had studied the photographs carefully, turning them this way and that. The man's appearance was quite different from that of the distinguished-looking Ferrari driver he had seen from time to time. And yet ... the likenesses were quite striking, and he had finally confirmed that it was, indeed, the Contessa's husband. Sergeant Sylvia immediately rang the Inspector with the news. She quickly organised her mother's schedule with a neighbour, got in her car and set off for the airport.

Landing in Spain, she was met by her opposite number, who drove them straight to the marina. They parked across the road and down the street from a pretty café, which she recognised from the photographs the Inspector had shown her.

"How did you find him?" Sylvia asked.

"He wasn't exactly living a low profile life," laughed her companion. "Once we had a fix on him, we clocked his movements, and I decided to make his acquaintance."

"So you've met him?" said Sylvia.

"Oh yes. We speak nearly every day. Of course, he doesn't realise I'm a police officer. He knows me as Mamen, the shy little waitress who serves him coffee and adores him from afar."

They both had a good chuckle at the eternal gullibility of men, the Italian and the Spaniard united in their view.

"What happens now?"

"We wait," responded Maria Carmen. "He's quite a creature of habit, and comes here most days at about the same time. I have a contact who usually rings me when the Maserati leaves the apartment block. If he turns right, then he'll be heading towards the fancy hotels to pick up one of his holiday paramours. I happen to know that his current squeeze is away at the moment, so if he turns left, he'll probably come to the café. The owner is an ex-policeman, and he understands my need to come and go. He doesn't know any details about the case. In fact, I only have the bare details myself. What is it he's done, exactly?"

"Right now, we're not entirely sure. All we know is that he attacked his wife and stole some very expensive items from their house, and the wife went missing shortly after reporting the crime to one of my officers. There has been no trace of her since; she could even be dead. Meanwhile he's been moving money around, and has tried to sell some of the stolen goods."

"Which is where we came in," said Maria Carmen. "But you know, he doesn't seem like the violent type to me. Although, in this job, you're never surprised at what people will get up to where money is concerned. He is certainly devious with a huge ego, but he operates more like a con artist than a thug. In fact, I think he's a bit of a softie where women are concerned. What's your view of his character?"

"I've never actually met him. All I have are reports from the wife who clearly loathes him, the views of the housekeeper who has a soft spot for him, and village gossip. It's not much to go on. But at the very least, he has a lot of questions to answer."

Maria Carmen's phone rang, and there followed a brief conversation in Spanish. She turned to Sylvia:

"The Maserati hasn't moved. Perhaps without the girlfriend he's decided to stay in the apartment this morning. Let's pay him a little visit."

"Should we call for back-up?"

"Nah," Maria Carmen laughed. "I think two strong women can handle a creep like him, don't you?" and they sped off towards their quarry.

Chapter 34

There was little sign of activity at the front of the palazzo. A few windows were open. Aurelia's Lamborghini was parked in the driveway as usual. He heard the sound of the lawn mower moving about behind the house. How they had argued about that mower. It was a fine sit-on machine, top of the range. Aurelia thought it was an extravagant luxury: *you are always so keen to spend my money on fripperies,* but Giancarlo insisted the staff should have proper equipment to work with: *would you have the man cut the grass with a pair of scissors?*

After a while he grew impatient, and telephoned the house.

"Pronto" was the response. It sounded like Josefina's voice, but Josefina always answered the phone in the elaborately formal way Aurelia insisted on. Something wasn't quite right.

Giancarlo disguised his accent. "Could I please speak to the Contessa." There was a hesitation at the other end.

"Who is calling?"

This wasn't what he'd planned. He thought quickly, and put as much authority into his new voice as he could muster. "It is a personal matter of great importance. Would you kindly put me through to the Contessa at once."

Again, the hesitation. What if Josefina recognised his voice?

"The Contessa is not here."

"When will she be back?"

"Excuse me, Signor. Perhaps you have not heard? I regret to inform you . . . The Contessa has been missing for some time.

"Missing?"

"Yes, Signor. There was a burglary at the palazzo and the Contessa went missing the same night. She hasn't been seen since."

Giancarlo was stunned. He didn't know what to say.

"The police were here, of course. They interviewed us and took all our fingerprints." Josefina filled the silence. "And it's been in all the papers, even on the television. There were helicopters hovering over the house, filming everything for the evening news. Did you not see it?"

"I ... I've been abroad," he stammered. "I didn't know. It's come as quite a shock."

"Well, I'm sorry to be the bearer of bad news, Signor. I don't know what else I can tell you. Shall I ask Officer Paulo to contact you? He usually comes here every week."

"No. Thank you. Please don't trouble yourself. I will contact the police directly. Thank you for your assistance."

He hung up. Slumped in his seat, Giancarlo tried to work out what on earth was going on.

Chapter 35

He was young, she had to admit. Perhaps 37, 38 ...? And good-looking. Ah, yes; that also was true. He was cultured and charming, he treated her with old-fashioned good manners, and her heart beat a little faster whenever she thought of him. *Be careful, Aurelia. Things may not be what they seem.*

And yet, oh but it was an intoxicating sensation, this falling in love. It made her feel fully alive. It was so long since she had noticed the patterns on butterfly wings, the aroma from pine trees warming in the sun. *You sound like a silly teenager. Don't make a spectacle of yourself.* No, she would not do that. She was a Contessa, with a fortune at her disposal, and she looked radiant, a good fifteen years younger than her age. She attracted admiration wherever she went. She could have any man. She was, in short, quite a catch. But still, there was Luiz Felipe.

Aurelia lay on the couch, eyes closed, while lithe young women wrapped her oiled body in warm towels, and smiled to herself. They were getting closer, she and Luiz Felipe. Her skin tingled whenever he accidentally brushed against it. Luiz Felipe hung on her every word. It was only a matter of time before they became intimate. A thrill of anticipation rippled through her body.

But Aurelia's instincts for self-preservation were always on guard. What did he see in her? What did he want from her? Over the weeks they had exchanged various bits of information about themselves, although Aurelia employed her usual policy of being generally truthful, but not too specific. Occasionally he had asked more searching questions, but when she flirtatiously changed the subject, he looked so much like a whipped puppy that she relented

somewhat and answered at least part of his question. He
never pushed her.

Could he be a gigolo? The Contessa had sharp antennae
for such men, and Luiz Felipe didn't fit the mould. He
seemed not to be particularly interested in her money, and
was always punctilious in picking up restaurant bills. She
liked that in him, a real gentleman. It delighted her to
politely decline and insist it was her turn. He was gracious
at all times. She had never bought him gifts, and he had
never given any indication that he wanted any.

Although habitually somewhat secretive about her own
circumstances, Aurelia was charmed by Luiz Felipe's
openness to all her questions. He worked in the family
business; they owned a string of hotels in the vast,
sprawling capital. He was in Rio to meet potential
partners for a new development along the coast. As the
only son, Luiz Felipe would take over the family business
once his father retired.

"But this day may never come," he smiled indulgently.
"He is 83 and has been talking about retiring for twenty
years. It's really my mother who wants him to slow down,
but we all know he wouldn't last long if he stopped
working. So my mother, my sisters and I had a family
conference and decided that I would look for a new
venture for my father to get his teeth into. It had to be on
the coast as my mother has long dreamed of living by the
ocean. If we can entice him to move to Rio, I will be able
to run our hotels back home without having to seek
permission for every little change I wish to make."

Aurelia had wondered why such an eligible man was still
single, and cast about to find a subtle way of raising the
topic. She needn't have worried; Luiz Felipe himself
brought it up. It seemed he had married too young, and
when the passion evaporated they had divorced. Since

then there had been several relationships, but none of them serious enough to commit to. His parents made no secret of their wish to see him marry again and settle down.

"Perhaps they long for grandchildren," ventured Aurelia.

"They already have too many," Luiz Felipe laughed. "My sisters are constantly breeding."

He talked easily, and was a good listener. Aurelia found herself hoping that his business discussions would take a very long time to reach their conclusion.

Chapter 36

Entering the apartment block, they came across an altercation in the lobby. Behind his desk the concierge stood with his arms folded, facing a soberly-dressed couple, the man gesticulating wildly and shouting at the concierge:

"What are you, a moron? Show us to the apartment immediately."

The woman with him tried to calm him down.

"I will not show you to the apartment, and if you don't shut up I'll come round there and shut you up," the concierge shouted back, beginning to roll up his sleeves.

"You seem incapable of understanding the simplest concepts. I've told you, the man has to be stopped."

"The only thing that's going to be stopped is your face when it meets my fist."

The two men squared up to each other.

Sergeant Maria Carmen decided it was time to put an end to all the posturing. She took out her badge and waved it in front of the men. "Right, what's going on here?"

The men spoke at the same time, each loudly listing the physical frailties of the other, as well as insulting their mothers, until Maria Carmen intervened once again. "Stop behaving like children, the pair of you, or I'll arrest you both and lock you in a cell till you've calmed down."

That got their attention.

"That's better. Now." She pointed at the man in a suit: "I don't want to hear another sound from you until I ask you a specific question. And you," she faced the concierge. "Tell me what this is about."

The concierge positively bristled with righteous indignation. "That idiot stormed in here demanding I let him into one of the apartments in my charge, even after I told him that the gentleman who lives there is away".

"Right." She turned to the man in the suit. "And what's your story?"

The man did his best to out-bristle the concierge. "The 'gentleman' in question is a thief and a con artist. I don't believe for a moment that he's away. His fancy car is still here in the parking area. I think this fool has been bribed to lie for him, and I insist on checking the apartment for myself."

The two men seemed about to square up to each other again, when the woman stepped forward.

"I believe I may be able to explain the situation, officer".

Maria Carmen tried to place her accent. "And you are?"

"I am a private investigator, and this is my client," she gestured to the man in the suit. "Officer, as this is a rather delicate matter, I wonder if we could sit down quietly and I will explain everything. I'm sure it can all be sorted out without further disturbance."

"Very well." At last, someone was talking sense. She glared at the concierge. "You will kindly wait in your office with the door shut while the rest of us have a little chat. I will tell you when you can come out."

The concierge was not happy. He resented being told what to do by a woman, and he really didn't like being kept out of the picture. But he recognised that there was little option, and sloped into the office, slamming the door loudly behind him. The two Sergeants Maria Carmen and Sylvia perched on the sofas near the desk, opposite the well-dressed couple.

"O.K." said Maria Carmen. "From the beginning."

The woman explained that her clients were a solicitor – she nodded to the man – and his uncle's cousin, an estate agent. The estate agent had sold a costly villa to an Italian male, the solicitor had drawn up the legal contract, the Italian had signed it and paid the usual deposit. Then he had simply disappeared without a word, leaving her clients with the obligation to pay the balance of the money for the villa. Money they did not have.

"We do not have it!" said the man, to emphasise the point.

At the mention of an Italian male, Maria Carmen exchanged a glance with Sylvia.

The woman continued. "I was hired to track down the Italian so that he could be brought to justice. When I was sure I'd found him, I asked my client to come and identify him to make absolutely certain, before having him arrested."

"And this Italian man's name is ... ?"

"Massio Maggiore" she replied.

Again the two officers exchanged glances, which the woman intercepted, saying "This man, I think you know?"

"And I think we need to discuss this matter at the station" said Maria Carmen.

The solicitor almost burst with suppressed fury. "But surely we must check his apartment first? His car is parked under the building, as has been verified by this lady". He pointed to the woman, who was looking closely at Maria Carmen. "I believe he is still here."

Maria Carmen walked swiftly behind the desk and pushed open the door, almost toppling the concierge standing immediately behind it. He assumed an innocent air.

"I have some questions for you, which you will answer truthfully. Is Señor Maggiore in his apartment?"

"No he is not."

"Do you know where he is?"

"He said he would be away for a few days, and I was to keep an eye out for his apartment and his car, in case anyone tried to rob him." The concierge gave a meaningful look at the solicitor.

"But he has robbed me!" The solicitor was beside himself. "We have to check his apartment immediately."

"We will do no such thing. This is private property, and without a search warrant we would be breaking the law. We will go to the station to sort this out."

They got up to leave, but when the concierge made to go with them, Maria Carmen pointed to the desk. "You will stay here and carry out your normal duties. When Señor Maggiore returns, you will telephone me immediately." She handed him a card. "And you will say nothing to the Señor about any of this. Is that clear?"

The concierge grunted, and Maria Carmen swept out of the door, the others following behind her.

Chapter 37

Parked in a quiet lane well away from the palazzo, Giancarlo opened his laptop and searched for the local papers. He scrolled down through the weeks, months, on and on past the usual stories that seemed to recur with depressing regularity: bureaucrats accused of taking bribes, fundraising for a new church roof, a pile-up on the by-pass. And there it was, a picture of himself, beside one of Aurelia, under the lurid headline: "Missing Contessa. Husband suspected of murder!"

He sat back in the seat and caught his breath. He tried to unravel the thoughts that collided with each other as they fired through his brain. Murder. He was suspected of murdering his wife. He quickly read the article, then read it again more slowly. The journalist speculated that Giancarlo had been caught by his wife in the act of stealing the family heirlooms, had beaten her, perhaps killed her, and then disposed of her body, which had not yet been found.

But he hadn't touched his wife, hadn't even been at the house when she returned from the clinic. His heart was racing. So where was Aurelia now? Had something happened to her? Had she been attacked and abducted by a stranger, perhaps? It was mystifying. He didn't particularly care about her welfare, but was very concerned that, in her absence, every finger pointed to him.

So that was why Josefina had answered the phone so informally, because Aurelia wasn't around to correct her sloppiness. Thank goodness he had disguised his voice. People would be looking for him, and though he believed Josefina preferred him to Aurelia, he knew she would be unable to resist the glory of being the first to report his re-appearance in the neighbourhood. And hadn't Josefina mentioned an Officer who went to the palazzo every week? It wasn't wise to stay in Italy. He would be much safer in Spain.

As he sped off to the border, his mind went over and over the last conversation he'd had with his wife. She'd been furious with him, of course, and without question she would seek revenge. But to do so she would first have to find him, and so far, she had not. As he was now known as Massio Maggiore, there was every likelihood she would never find him. Nor did any of it explain her disappearance, the presence of her blue Lamborghini outside the palazzo, her continued absence all this time later.

Nothing made any sense to him, other than the imperative of getting back to Spain as fast as possible, where he could sit quietly and think it all through. Until he understood what was going on, it was impossible to know whether it was safer to be Massio Maggiore or Giancarlo di Tramonti. In fact, it might be wise to have passports in both names, and use whichever suited the circumstances. His powerful survival instinct sent him on a detour.

Chapter 38

By the time they reached the police station, the solicitor had managed to calm down. The two sergeants, the solicitor and the private investigator sat round a small table in an interview room.

"Now," Sergeant Maria Carmen turned to the woman, "I am interested in this Massio Maggiore. Tell me about him."

The private investigator delved into her handbag. "I can show you a picture". All four leant forward to scrutinise the image. Again, Maria Carmen and Sylvia exchanged glances, and once more the private investigator caught the look. "But I think already you two know him," she said.

"Right now, I'm more interested in how you know him."

"It seems he thought he was being clever by using different hire cars to visit my clients. But they were suspicious of him from the start, and took the precaution of noting the hire company and car registration."

"We were cleverer than him," beamed the solicitor.

Maria Carmen turned to him. "Why were you suspicious?"

"Because he seemed to have no permanent address, and always preferred to deal in cash."

"Then why did you not raise this matter with the authorities?"

The solicitor's neck wriggled from side to side. This was not going the way he intended. "The fact is he is a crook, and we are raising the matter now," he burbled.

Maria Carmen signalled for the private investigator to continue.

The woman shrugged. "It was not so difficult to track him down, but his appearance was different from the description given to me by my clients. Therefore, I decided it would be necessary to make his acquaintance and see what I could dig up."

"And?"

"He gave every sign of a comfortable lifestyle, but without having any obvious source of income. I watched him for a while, and quickly realised that he made a living by preying on women visiting the resort. They were sometimes alone, sometimes with female friends, but there were never any husbands present, and the women always had access to money, plenty of money. Each 'affair' lasted only a relatively short time, ending when the women would return to their usual lives. When I spotted a gap, I set about introducing myself."

The two women studied each other for a while. Finally, Sergeant Maria Carmen said: "You are Klaar."

"Yes. And you are Mamen."

"You look different from the 'Klaar' in the hotel. She wears a lot more bling."

"And you are not so like the poor little waitress."

"We were both trying to catch a thief. I think we succeeded."

The three women laughed, while the solicitor looked from one to the other, trying to work out what was going on.

"What's going on?" he said out loud, but nobody paid him any attention.

Klaar nodded towards Sylvia. "I do not know this lady."

"I am Sergeant Sylvia from the Italian police. I have come to interview this 'Massio', whose real name is Giancarlo. His wife, the Contessa Aurelia di Tramonti, was attacked and robbed in the family palazzo. Many valuable items were stolen. Neither Giancarlo nor the Contessa has been seen since. We suspect she may have been murdered."

Klaar's brow furrowed. "Really? Well. To me he does not seem the type to murder. More like a needy boy who has failed to grow up."

Maria Carmen conceded the point. "I felt the same. And yet, there is no explanation for the missing Contessa."

"So what happens now?" asked Sergeant Sylvia.

"As his fancy car is still here, in all likelihood he will return shortly. When he does, we will pull him in for questioning."

The solicitor was beside himself. "What about my money?" he wailed.

"Oh we will ask him about that, too. He has a lot of questions to answer."

Chapter 39

Back once more in the safety of his apartment, Giancarlo poured himself a drink and sank into an armchair. He must think, and quickly. He was on the run for something he didn't do. At least, he didn't do the part that involved murdering his wife. This whole thing must be some trick of Aurelia's. She was bound to strike at him somehow, and he needed to work out exactly what she was up to.

He didn't believe she knew where he was, otherwise she would have sent in a couple of pumped up thugs to give him a kicking. It was more likely that she was trying to flush him out from wherever he was hiding. Yes, that was it. If he made a run for it, someone would notice and might tell the wrong people. Perhaps it was better to sit tight. Wait till the storm clouds passed. Besides, he really didn't want to give up the profitable and pleasant life he had built for himself. Like all the others, Klaar was shaping up nicely, and only needed a tiny push before indulging him with a trinket or two.

And then there was Mamen. She had become precious to him. The thought of never seeing her again was intolerable. He pictured her shy, serious little face. With his wealth and taste there were so many ways he could improve her life. He shook his head; no, he could not abandon Mamen.

Deep in thought, he jumped at the sudden knock on his door. It must be that fool of a concierge, although he usually rang before coming up. Giancarlo peered through the spyhole. Two burly policemen stood outside, with a third smaller person he couldn't see properly. He gasped a curse, before realising that they would hear the sound and know he was there. He swung round, desperately looking for a way out, but there was only the balcony, and it was too high up to jump. The knocking resumed, and a voice called out:

"Signor Maggiore. We know you are there. Kindly open the door." It was a woman, speaking to him in Italian.

Because he couldn't think of any other course of action, he slowly pulled back the door. A brassy-looking woman with peroxide hair stepped forward, holding out her badge. The two policemen filled the doorway.

"My name is Sergeant Sylvia. I am a police officer and I am investigating the disappearance of the Contessa Aurelia di Tramonti. I believe you may be able to help with our enquiries, and would request that you come to the police station at once."

With all the dignity he could muster he thundered: "Are you arresting me?"

"No, Signor Maggiore. I am merely inviting you to accompany me to the police station to answer a few questions."

He nodded towards the policemen, "Then why are those two here?"

"They are here to make sure we don't get lost on the way to the station. After all," Sylvia smiled innocently, "they are Spanish; they know the roads better than you or I."

Chapter 40

He was led into a room that looked like every interview room from all the crime films he had ever seen. There was even the obligatory two-way mirror. Giancarlo almost laughed. What a cliché. The peroxide Sergeant asked him to state his name, date of birth and address.

On the other side of the mirror, Maria Carmen nodded to the solicitor. "Well?"

"Yes, that's him. He's changed, but I wouldn't forget that voice, that arrogant tilt of the head as though he's having a huge joke at everyone's expense. Are you going to arrest him?"

"I would like you to wait outside while he is questioned," she responded. "I will come and take your statement later."

Sergeant Sylvia opened her laptop and positioned it on the table so that Giancarlo could see the screen. She clicked through a series of pictures showing the palazzo from several angles and asked him if he recognised it. He did not. She clicked onto a photograph of the Contessa. Did he know her? He did not. She brought up images of the Contessa's ransacked bedroom. He blinked several times, saying nothing, but wondering what on earth had happened in that bedroom. He braced himself, knowing that it would not be long before the Italian Sergeant showed him a picture of the Contessa's husband. When it came, he didn't move a muscle.

Behind the glass, Maria Carmen watched him closely. He was a study in self-control, his face devoid of expression, his body relaxed .... but under the table his right leg jiggled nervously throughout. It was time to unsettle him even further. She breezed into the room with a broad smile. "Ciao, Giancarlo." He glanced her way, looked back at the screen, then did a double take as he brought her features into view. Maria Carmen leaned towards the screen. "Oh, I forgot, you now call yourself Massio, Massio Maggiore. But the likeness is unmistakable, don't you think, Giancarlo?"

His face was a parody of appalled confusion, his mouth opening and closing like a fish. Finally, he was able to muster one word. "Mamen?"

"Well, officially speaking my name is Maria Carmen and I am an officer in the Spanish police force. But you may call me Mamen if you like. And I'll call you Giancarlo, if that's alright with you?"

Sylvia was mightily impressed with Maria Carmen's tactics. Giancarlo was unable to form the words that raced round his head. Studying his face, the two police women could almost see the cogs in his mind as he struggled to process the revelations of the previous few minutes. But all he could do was to repeat "Mamen?"

"Yes, we have established that. And now we need to establish that you are Giancarlo, the lady in the pictures is your wife, the Contessa Aurelia di Tramonti, and the palazzo is your home. Si?"

Too late, Giancarlo realised that he had missed the moment when he might still be able to blag his way out of the trap they had set. Indeed, he could think of nothing, save that Mamen, his little Mamen whom he had wanted to protect like a daughter, had deceived him. It was as though all the air had been sucked from his body. He slumped in the chair, and nodded.

"Thank you, Giancarlo." She indicated Sylvia. "Now this officer has come a long way to meet you. She has a number of questions to ask you about events in Italy. And when she has finished, I have a few questions of my own to put to you about a certain property near Barcelona." Barcelona? What was she talking about? He couldn't think straight. His mind was being buffeted by raging seas, with no land in sight, and not even a piece of driftwood to cling onto. The peroxide Sergeant was talking, but he was unable to take it in and she had to repeat the request.

"My Inspector would like to conduct a preliminary interview with you via skype. Would you be willing to do this?"

What real choice did he have?

Chapter 41

At first, he admitted nothing, not even to being the Giancarlo in the picture. His plan was to stall until he found out exactly what was going on. The Italian Inspector played the same game, asking many questions without revealing any details of the 'incident' he was investigating. This stalemate threatened to continue indefinitely, until Maria Carmen went into another room and phoned the Inspector.

She explained that she had been watching unobserved while Sergeant Sylvia showed Giancarlo the pictures. "The thing I noticed was that he seemed genuinely surprised to see the state of the Contessa's bedroom. He is clearly a very good liar, but could barely contain his reaction to the ransacked room."

"And what does this suggest to you?"

"That when he left the palazzo, the wife's room had been intact. Which poses the question: who did ransack the room, and why?"

"Yes, indeed" murmured the Inspector. Then, noticing her hesitation, "Anything else?"

"Well, Inspector, both Klaar and I – Sergeant Sylvia has explained Klaar's role in all this?"

"She has. Please go on."

"Well Klaar and I got quite close to Giancarlo, and we both separately formed the opinion that he was not a violent man. It's only an opinion, of course."

114

"Thank you for your insights, Sergeant. They are most helpful."

Returning to the interview room, Maria Carmen found herself envying Sylvia her courteous and open-minded boss.

The short break confirmed to Giancarlo that it was imperative he find out what crimes he was being accused of without admitting who he was. He was forming an intricate, and he thought rather clever, strategy for doing so when the Inspector returned to the screen.

"Giancarlo," he began, "for we know you are Giancarlo, you have two choices in front of you. Either you admit your identity and return with Sergeant Sylvia to Italy voluntarily for further questioning. Or I will ask our most helpful Spanish colleagues to detain you while I arrange a warrant for your arrest."

Giancarlo puffed out his chest in a show of bravado. "On what charge?"

"Charge? Oh Giancarlo, not 'charge'. Rather multiple 'charges'. We begin with robbery, and selling stolen goods. We then move on to abduction, and murder."

"Murder? Abduction? This is ridiculous. Who am I supposed to have murdered?"

"Your wife."

"My wife?" Giancarlo's mind raced back to the photographs of Aurelia's dishevelled bedroom. There must be some terrible mistake. "But my wife was alive and well when I last saw her," he blurted out, before registering their self-satisfied smiles.

"Then I am sure you will be only too happy to help us with our enquiries into her whereabouts."

Giancarlo shut his mouth and folded his arms. He would say nothing more.

The Inspector pressed home his advantage. "Do I take it that you agree to accompany Sergeant Sylvia back to Italy in order to clear up this – confusion?"

Giancarlo unfolded, and then refolded his arms.

"Or would you prefer to remain in custody in Spain?"

Giancarlo waved a dismissive arm.

"Thank you."

Chapter 42

Wasn't technology amazing? You could be anywhere in the world and still be in touch with everywhere else. Aurelia had never thought of herself as being computer-savvy, but these days it was all so simple. You tapped a few keys, clicked a few links, and hey presto! The world was brought right to you. Luiz Felipe had shown her how.

Sitting in her favourite café sipping a delicious cappuccino, she browsed through pictures from the Milan catwalk. If there was one thing she missed, it was Italian style. The French had a reputation for fashion, it was true. But they seemed obsessed by stick-thin women who looked like boys. Some of the designs she studied were positively freakish and just made her gasp with astonishment; they were only wearable by emaciated 14 year-olds. But then there were the Italian classics: beautiful colours, exquisite fabrics, shaped to flatter real, curvy women.

A young waitress breezed by to see if she wanted anything, and her eyes were transfixed by the screen. Aurelia smiled up at her, "What do you think?"

"Gorgeous – but too expensive for a humble waitress!" she laughed.

"You never know. One day a fantastic opportunity could come your way." Aurelia's mind produced a picture she hadn't thought of in years. Her first paid job, cleaning the same bathrooms day after day in the town's only hotel, until the time a lonely businessman came to stay. "When your chance comes, you have to take advantage of it immediately."

"I'll bear that in mind," the waitress smiled, but she didn't seem convinced, and moved off to check another table.

My Portuguese must be improving. But it was hard work at this early stage, and she knew her accent was still strongly Italian.

On a whim, Aurelia went to her 'Favourites' list, scrolled down to 'Italian newspapers' and clicked on the nationals. A few minutes' browsing told her that it was all the usual drivel, nothing much to hold her attention. *Might as well see what's happening back at the ranch.* She clicked on the regional paper. Seemingly endless corruption scandals took centre stage, accompanied by photographs of silver-haired politicians and teenage 'models'. Not much different from the national papers.

Sipping coffee, her eye was caught by a headline: *Husband questioned about murdered Contessa.* This was much more interesting. There were several contessas in the region. The ones she had met were loathsome, and Aurelia wondered which one of them had been murdered, almost praying that it was that awful snob Livia, who thought she was better than the others because she'd been born an aristocrat. Then Aurelia saw her own name, and almost choked. Murder? She quickly scanned the article. It described her as being violently assaulted in her home, and having disappeared without trace, thus leading the police to suspect murder. It went on to say that her husband had returned to Italy from abroad and was 'helping the police with their enquiries'. The police refused to say whether he was the main suspect, but the journalist had no such scruples, asserting that "the culprit is likely to be charged in the next few days".

Aurelia sat back and let out a breath. *Well! They think Giancarlo has murdered me.* Her first impulse was one of triumph. She thought again of that awful phone call from her husband, spitting out exactly what he thought of her and gloating over his deviousness. *So, Giancarlo, I bet that's taken the wind out of your sails. That's what happens to men who deceive and rob their wives and think they can just walk away. Let's see how you try and wriggle out of this one. Bastardo!*

"Ciao"

Aurelia looked up, startled, as Luiz Felipe planted a kiss on the top of her head and plonked himself down on the chair next to hers.

"I thought I might find you here." He glanced at the screen. "Getting homesick?" He reached to angle the screen his way. Aurelia was fairly certain that Luiz Felipe didn't read Italian, but he might well recognise her from the grainy photographs.

"Oh, that - it's just silly nonsense." She leaned forward and gently shut the laptop, pulling it towards her. "I was looking at some fashion pictures, and just got sidetracked."

Luiz Felipe looked at her. "I'm serious, Aurelia. You're not thinking of deserting me, are you? I thought you liked it here."

"Darling, I *love* it here. I love everything about Rio: the climate, the music, the people – one person in particular." She bestowed on him her most winning smile. "I have no intention of leaving."

"But you must miss Italy. It is your home, after all. I would miss Brazil."

"There are one or two things I miss. Being able to speak Italian wherever I go, for one; except with you, of course." She smiled at him, and he gave a mock bow. "And of
119

course, I have business connections there which I must keep an eye on. But apart from that, my home is now here, in Rio. I don't want to be anywhere else."

He reached for her hand, kissed it gently, and cradled it in his as he looked deep into her eyes. "I'm so glad."

They remained like this for some moments, just gazing at each other. Then suddenly, Luiz Felipe jumped. "I have a fantastic idea."

Aurelia laughed. She loved this almost childlike spontaneity in him, so different from her natural inclination to plot and plan. No doubt he would announce some madcap adventure, hopefully something more sedate than his recent suggestion of paragliding. "Tell me."

"Why don't we both go to Italy?"

The smile froze on her face. "What?"

"Wow." He laughed and shook her hands. "I've really caught you off guard, haven't I? I was beginning to think that wasn't possible."

"But why go to Italy?"

"Why not? It's where you're from, and you obviously miss it or you wouldn't be reading Italian newspapers. And as you say, you still have business interests there, so why don't we take a short holiday, and you can show me where you live. I could meet your family."

"I have no family."

"But you have a home, surely. Everyone has a home. And I'd like to see it."

Chapter 43

The photographs they had shown him bore little relation to the room he was now standing in, which had clearly been tidied and polished by Josefina. The Inspector and Sergeant Sylvia had walked him round the house, asking him to identify what was missing. He gave every impression of being so dazed and shaken that he was unable to answer their questions, and this was only partly an act. Obviously he knew what he had taken from the house, but he realised that other things were missing as well, things he hadn't touched. He couldn't work it out. Was it possible that the palazzo had been burgled the very night Aurelia had arrived home, just hours after he himself had stolen her things? Surely that would be too big a coincidence.

They told him that the Contessa had been attacked, which their own officer could verify. They wheeled him in, too, this officer. Officer Paulo, overawed by his superiors, and stumbling over his words in an effort to abide by earlier instructions to answer only the questions put by the Inspector. Giancarlo thought him a fool. But still, he was a police officer, and his testimony would carry much weight.

None of it made sense to Giancarlo. How could any of this be? The only person who knew exactly what he'd taken was lying dead at the bottom of a gorge. Unless that little rat Fredo had taken it into his head to make some extra money on the side. Perhaps he had followed Aurelia into the house, beaten her up, threatened to come back and finish her off if she called the police, and then made off with her jewellery and cash. He certainly seemed capable of such thuggery. But the timing didn't work out. Would Fredo have been able to do all that, and yet get to the gorge before him? Besides, if Fredo had wanted more he could easily have driven off with the van full of paintings, and not bothered to turn up for his rendezvous at the gorge. Giancarlo could hardly have reported him to the police. It didn't add up.

Giancarlo needed to think, to sort out his story. If he told the police exactly what had happened, it would go some way to proving that he hadn't murdered his wife. On the other hand, it would also prove that he had indeed robbed his wife, murdered his accomplice, and subsequently lived off the profits of stolen goods. What on earth could he say in his defence that didn't also incriminate him? Somehow he had to buy time so that he could work it out. He started panting, clutched his arm and then his heart, and sank to his knees. He knew they would suspect this was a trick, but perhaps this modern culture of health and safety meant they would have to get him to hospital, just in case. It was worth a try.

He needn't have bothered. Sergeant Sylvia announced that she was a qualified first-aider. She laid him in the recovery position, assuring her Inspector that she and Officer Paulo could take turns to apply mouth-to-mouth resuscitation if necessary while they waited for the ambulance to turn up. Giancarlo was appalled at the prospect, but had no choice but to play along. When the ambulance arrived, Sergeant Sylvia went with him to the hospital, where he was declared fully recovered, and returned to the police station.

"Well?" the Inspector raised an eyebrow.

"I think I would like to speak to my lawyer," said Giancarlo.

"I think that would be very wise," he replied.

Chapter 44

It was a side of him she hadn't seen before: the petulant child, spoilt from birth, and angry when his wishes weren't fulfilled. He had called her "secretive" when she avoided answering further questions about her background, and "suspicious" when all he was trying to do was to "get closer" to her.

"I tell you everything. But when I ask you the simplest thing, I am met with evasions."

"I am not being evasive, Luiz Felipe. It's just that there is very little to tell you that you don't already know."

"I don't know where you call home, apart from 'somewhere in Italy'."

"I am from a small town in the north-east of Italy. But my home is now here, in Rio. Or at least, I'd like it to be."

"So why can't we go to this 'small town in the north-east of Italy'? What is the big secret that you want to keep from me?"

Aurelia sighed. "There is no big secret. But I have no need to go there at the moment. I can quite easily manage my affairs from here." His furious expression did not alter, and she tried another tack. "Of course, I may well have to return to Italy in a few months time to attend to some business interests. Perhaps we can think about going later in the year?" *And perhaps you will have forgotten by then*, she thought, but did not say.

He pulled a face. "This is not about your business interests. It's about trust. How much you trust me. And it's evident that you don't!"

They had had this conversation, or at least something very like it, two or three times. It always ended the same way, with Luiz Felipe storming off in a huff. She would usually allow a day or so for him to cool off, and then they would make it up, until whenever the subject was next raised. But this time his voice had been harsher, more accusing, and several days had elapsed without a word. Her dismay at his behaviour was compounded by the fact that she had always, somewhere deep inside, expected things to turn out this way. It had surely been too good to last.

Aurelia picked up the phone and pressed the keys. A recorded message told her the number was no longer in service. She tried again in case she'd pressed the wrong button. Same response. This was strange. He must have changed his number. He'd never done that before. She supposed this was some new tactic designed to throw her off guard. Well, it would take more than that to unsettle the Contessa Aurelia di Tramonti. She would simply wait. *He'll come back.* She told herself. *He always does.*

It was a measure of how much time they had been spending together that she now found herself at something of a loose end. She sat on her balcony, a cool glass in her hand, gazing out at the colourful promenade, the beach that always seemed to be full of young people frolicking and flirting (*where did they keep the old people?*), the shimmering ocean. She sipped her wine, looking along the coast to the north, and then turned to look towards the south. It was a view that still entranced her.

Luiz Felipe would contact her sooner or later. She would be magnanimous. Perhaps there was some trinket she could give him. He came from a well-off family, of

124

course, but even so she thought he would respond to a little something in gold. In her experience, men were very predictable, at least all the men she had ever known. When they behaved like fretful children, they could always be distracted with presents. She had learnt this early on in life, when she had no money and the only gift she possessed was herself. It was a trick that had gone on working long after she became wealthy, even late into her years with Giancarlo.

Ah yes. Giancarlo. *I wonder what developments there have been.* She opened her laptop and clicked on her local newspaper. Bold headlines proclaimed, "Murdered Contessa: husband arrested". She read the article quickly. It was full of speculation, short on facts, asserting that "the husband had a history of violence" (not really true), that he had "made millions from selling her pictures" (ridiculous, since most of them were fake), and that "Police were hopeful of finding the Contessa's body within days" (what body?). So this was getting serious.

Aurelia was surprised to realise how hard her heart was pounding, and tried to work out why. She had persuaded herself that Giancarlo deserved all he got, so surely she couldn't be concerned for his welfare? Of course, it had never occurred to her that he could be charged with murder, and locked away for decades. She had wanted to punish him, but this would be a little extreme. Besides, her wonderful new life inclined her to be less vengeful. And yet, her heart was still battering away.

What to do? What if she simply turned up in Italy, seemingly unaware of all the fuss arising from her absence? An argument between husband and wife that had got out of hand. All just a misunderstanding. They would have to let him go. But then, she would have to explain how she had managed to leave Italy without using her passport. It probably wasn't a grave offence and she was not particularly worried about how it would be viewed by the police. Of much greater concern was the reaction of the men who had helped her, if she were pressed to reveal how she had done it. No, that would not end well.

And then there was the publicity. Italians loved a scandal, particularly if it involved aristocrats and money. The story might be picked up by the international media. Luiz Felipe was always glued to his electronic gadgets and was bound to spot it, and her little romantic idyll would come crashing down around her.

Yes, that was what made her heart pound so. Luiz Felipe must not be allowed to come across the story before she had a chance to prepare him. He was a man of the world and would surely take it in his stride, even perhaps find it amusing. What he would not enjoy would be her concealing her background from him. She must speak to him.

She tried his number once more, and predictably got the same response. She rang his hotel, but they said his name was not on the guest list. She asked them to check again, perhaps he had recently moved out, but they assured her he had never stayed there. This was odd since they had dined at least twice in the hotel's restaurant, and she had been charmed at his insistence on paying the bill.

When she thought about it, they had spent most of the time either out and about, or in her apartment, Luiz Felipe declaring that it was much nicer there than his sterile hotel room. She bit her lip, wondering how on earth to contact him, when it dawned on her to look him up on the internet.

Typing in his name, she clicked on the link that brought up the family's history. It was, of course, written in Portuguese, but fortunately Luiz Felipe had shown her how to get these things translated. It was all there, the whole story complete with photographs of the smiling family: the patriarch and matriarch from humble beginnings, the string of hotels in the capital, several daughters and numerous grandchildren.

And then: "Luiz Felipe, the only son and heir to the family fortune, tragically died in a speedboat accident five years ago."

Chapter 45

"In my professional opinion, this is your best strategy."

Giancarlo sniffed. *Best for whom?*

"Of course, if you are determined to sacrifice yourself on the altar of principle, then there is nothing more to be said."

Puffed up, pompous, supercilious oaf, talking down to him as if he were a half-wit. Lawyers!

They had discussed his predicament for two hours. To the lawyer it was a simple matter of expediency: better to admit to theft and serve a short sentence, than be tried for murder and risk a much longer prison term. But Giancarlo didn't see why he should go to prison at all. He much preferred his own strategy: deny that he had stolen anything, insist that he and his wife had decided to go their separate ways and, rather than involve grasping lawyers in their affairs, had settled on a financial arrangement whereby Giancarlo would take an agreed list of items from the palazzo. The fact that many of these items had turned out to be fakes meant that he, Giancarlo, was the victim, not his wife.

Besides, Giancarlo had not been entirely frank with his lawyer, thinking it prudent to avoid any mention of Fredo, and how he came to be lying at the bottom of a gorge. There was no reason to confuse things with that particular detail. He decided the best approach was to assert that as he hadn't stolen anything from his wife, let alone murdered her, there was nothing to admit to. Aurelia wasn't around to contradict whatever he said, and if she turned up at some point in the future, well he'd jump off that particular bridge when he came to it.

"But, Signor, you have overlooked some rather important pieces of evidence," the lawyer's obvious smugness made Giancarlo want to punch him. "For instance, you are forgetting about Officer Paulo."

"Officer Paulo is a fool."

"That may well be, but he is an official fool, and his testimony will be taken seriously."

"Well if that's all the evidence they have …"

"Then there is the state of the Contessa's bedroom."

Ah, yes. He would need an explanation for that.

"My wife is incredibly untidy by nature. She also has a strong sense of her position. As a Contessa, she doesn't believe in doing anything that servants could do. Clothes are simply left where they fall; anything dropped on the floor stays there until someone else picks it up. Josefina will verify that."

"And the open safe? Is that left for Josefina to tidy up, too?"

"There is probably a perfectly simple explanation."

"Such as?"

"How would I know? I wasn't there. I can't explain any of it – the room, Aurelia's apparent 'disappearance' – because I simply wasn't there. And no-one can prove otherwise."

They danced around the same issues for a while, until the lawyer threw up his hands. "Very well. You are the client. It is not what I advise, but the decision is yours."

Giancarlo inclined his head, rather magnanimously he thought.

"However, I regret I will not be able to represent you myself. One of my colleagues will take your case. Do not be disconcerted by her youthful appearance. She is highly efficient, and I'm sure you will not be disappointed."

I'm sure I won't. She couldn't fail to be a great improvement on you.

Chapter 46

She opened the door to find him grinning that boyish smile, a bottle of champagne in his hand.

"Aurelia – or should I say, Contessa". He made an elaborate bow.

She attempted to slam the door in his face, but he jammed it open with his foot, waving the bottle. "I thought we could have a little celebration together."

"Get away from my door or I will call the concierge to eject you."

"You're bound to be upset, but I can explain everything. If you let me in we can have a very civilised, and may I say profitable, discussion."

"I have nothing to discuss with you. I don't even know who you are."

"Aurelia, do you really want to have this conversation on the doorstep?"

She hesitated, and then released the door. She watched in astonishment as he calmly strode to the kitchen, put the bottle in the fridge, and then sat down, gesturing for her to join him. "Who the hell are you? You're not Luiz Felipe. He's dead."

"Yes, I'm sorry about the deception. But it was necessary to get to the truth."

"What truth?"

"That you are the Contessa Aurelia di Tramonti, currently missing from her Italian palazzo, and presumed dead."

"I know who I am. Who are you?"

"My name is Tomas Santos. Here is my card."

She declined to take it, so he placed it on the coffee table between them.

"I am a freelance journalist." He saw her wince. "I am working for a syndicate of magazines available across pretty much the whole of South America. Our readers will be very interested in your story."

"And what exactly is my story?"

"You are a glamorous, wealthy aristocrat living in a beautiful palazzo in far-off Europe. You reported to the police that you were attacked by your husband, who stole many of your possessions: money, jewels, paintings, etc. – a long list of expensive items. That same evening you disappeared without trace. Your husband was nowhere to be found. Eventually the police concluded that he had kidnapped you, taken you somewhere to murder you, and disposed of your body. It took some searching, but finally he was tracked down living in Spain, having altered his name and his appearance. He is now back in Italy, shortly to be charged with your murder."

Tomas relaxed back into his armchair.

"It is a fantastic story, don't you think? But of course, you are not actually dead. You are alive and well, living 4,000 miles away from home, and looking much more beautiful than in those raggedy old photos the police issued."

Aurelia didn't move; her lips were set tight and she was breathing heavily. "What do you want?"

"To know what really happened the day you were – attacked."

"Why on earth would I say anything to a journalist?"

"Aurelia, just think about this for a moment. I know who you are. I am aware that you built an elaborate fiction around your disappearance from Italy. I also know that you seem quite prepared to allow your husband to be charged with a very serious crime he didn't commit: namely, your murder. And I begin to wonder why. The obvious answer seems to be some sort of revenge. Now, I am intrigued. I would like to understand this revenge: what caused it; how far you are prepared to let things go. For instance, are you willing to see your husband sent to prison, perhaps for years?"

She turned her head and glared out of the window, remaining silent.

"In my trade, you get to meet all sorts of people, often sordid, seedy people, and you don't strike me as the sort of woman who would go quite that far."

She snorted. Men always thought they knew her.

"But even if you were prepared to sacrifice your husband's liberty, I, in all conscience, would not be prepared to do so."

"Conscience?" she snapped.

"Yes indeed, Aurelia. I could not stand by and let a man go to prison for a crime he didn't commit. Nor would my editor permit me to do so. If you allowed a trial to go ahead, I would be obliged to print what I have uncovered, to expose your actions to the public gaze." He leant forward, his face a mask of sincerity. "But I really don't want to do that, Aurelia. Not without giving you a fair chance to present your side of the story."

She turned back to face him.

"So, now we are getting to it. You are a second-rate hack who has stumbled across a juicy story and wants to make money out of it. Well, this isn't a 'story' to entertain your readers. This is about real people's lives."

He bridled. "For the record, I am not a second-rate hack, as you put it. I am a professional who commands the highest fees for my journalism. My work is disseminated across continents. And I will publish your story whether you agree to it or not."

She folded her arms.

"Listen, Aurelia. This could be a golden opportunity for both of us. There will be articles, a book, perhaps even a T.V. programme. We could make our fortunes."

"I already have a fortune."

"True. But if I expose you as a liar and a fraud, how long do you think it would take the Italian authorities to come for you? You would have to leave Rio, and I know how much you love it here. And if they put you in jail, what good would your fortune be to you then?"

"But I have done nothing wrong. I have broken no laws. There would be no grounds for arresting me. This has all been a ridiculous misunderstanding."

"Then collaborate with me in explaining this 'misunderstanding' to my readers. It truly is in your best interests, Aurelia."

"On the contrary, my best interest is to remain silent."

"Then I would have no choice but to print what I know."

Chapter 47

"My name is Daniela Domossola." The young woman leaned forward to proffer her hand, silken curls sliding over her shoulder. "We met briefly once before, but in all the hurly burly of your return to Italy you may well have forgotten?"

"I could never forget such a beautiful face."

Her brief smile was cautious, as if accustomed to flattery and not willing to fall for it.

"I have been appointed your legal representative by my superior, but I must point out that you are entirely at liberty to find an alternative lawyer should you wish."

Giancarlo wondered what cataclysm could possibly induce him to wish for an alternative to this gorgeous creature.

"You don't have to make that decision right away. I suggest that we discuss your situation, during which I will outline my proposal for handling your case, after which you can make up your mind. I have been fully briefed and have a number of questions for you."

He lifted a hand to signal that she should begin.

"My first question is to ask how you would like to be addressed. I am aware that your wife is a Contessa, and assumed you would therefore be a Conte, but all the paperwork refers to you as Signor."

"That is correct. My wife married into the title and made sure she kept hold of it when her first husband died. She is a woman of great foresight and ambition. I wanted to be addressed as Conte when we married, but Aurelia insisted this was not legally possible. I should have been firmer in pressing my case, but I was young and in love ... what can one do?" He shrugged. "But you may call me Giancarlo."

She took him through the main facts of his case, looking up from her papers occasionally to seek his confirmation. Giancarlo merely nodded from time to time.

"You are aware, Signor di Tramonti ..."

"'Giancarlo', please" he interrupted.

"Perhaps we should remain on a formal basis at this preliminary stage." This was said firmly. "Signor di Tramonti, you are aware that my superior recommended you plead guilty to theft as the safer option."

Giancarlo indicated his disgust at such a preposterous notion.

She continued, "Of course, he is entirely correct. That would indeed be the safer option. However, I believe that the alternative approach, if carefully handled, would be achievable."

He sat up straighter. If she hadn't before, Signorina Domossola now had his full attention.

"It seems to me that the evidence put forward by the police is entirely circumstantial: there is no actual proof that it was you who attacked your wife, or that you took anything from the palazzo without her permission. Unless your wife comes forward to say something different or, god forbid, her body is found, then the case against you is very weak."

That puffed-up fool of a lawyer. He clearly couldn't even be bothered to try.

"I must emphasise, Signor di Tramonti, that there is significant risk involved. Their case may be very weak, but a clever lawyer could craft it into something much stronger."

"Are you not also a clever lawyer, Signorina?"

She gave him a level look. "I am a very good lawyer, Signor, and I believe that we could win our case. But if we lose, the consequences for you are much greater than for me. There is no doubt that you would be sent to prison for several years. Therefore, you must think very carefully before making your decision."

She assembled her papers and put them in her briefcase. "I will return tomorrow." As she stood up, her long, chestnut hair swung out behind her.

"Signorina, please sit down." He straightened his cuffs rather theatrically. "I have made my decision. I want you to take them on."

Still standing, she stared at him without a trace of softness in her face. "Are you absolutely sure, Signor? Once we file our plea there can be no going back."

Giancarlo had always been a gambler. He would be spending a great deal of time with Daniela Domossola. How delightful. It was worth the risk.

Chapter 48

They talked. Or rather, Tomas talked ... on and on. She remained silent, staring out of the window. After a while he went to the fridge and poured them both champagne. Once more he explained his plan, involving agents and book deals, figures and copyright, contacts in television. He seemed to have it all worked out. Her glass sat untouched. He tried flattery, then baby-talk. Eventually, he sighed.

"Aurelia. What can I say to persuade you that this will be your best option?"

She looked at him. "Nothing. Because it is not my best option. Though I can see it's yours!" Her gaze returned to the window.

A golden sun began to sink behind the mountain, so that he saw her in silhouette, a fine-looking woman.

"Aurelia, we need to sort this out today. Please allow me to take you to dinner so that we may talk further. You can't have failed to notice that I have a very generous allowance." If this was an attempt at humour, it backfired. She turned to face him, "You are a liar and a cheat, and I would choke on every mouthful."

Tomas put his head in his hands, pushing his fingers through his hair to try to quash his rising anger.

"Very well, Aurelia. For the last time, let me spell out precisely what will happen next if we cannot reach an amicable agreement. Tonight I will complete the article I have drafted. Tomorrow I will take it to my editor. I should warn you that he already has a somewhat lurid headline in mind to attract our dear readers, alongside some rather fetching pictures: the Contessa shopping for jewellery in the most fashionable and expensive stores; the Contessa on the massage table barely covered by a towel."

She looked at him in horror. At last he was getting through to her.

"The article and pictures will be published in the next edition, a double-page spread in glorious colour. After which, it will only be a matter of days, perhaps even hours, before the police are knocking on your door. I will be there to record your departure from Brazil, and your arrival in Italy. Before you have time to catch your breath you will be interviewed by a high-ranking police officer, so anxious to learn how you departed your native land without leaving a trace that he might feel obliged to detain you immediately. Things will very swiftly spiral out of control."

She seemed to sag a little.

"But it needn't be like this, Aurelia. If you and I can sit and discuss the possibilities like two sensible people, I can make so much of it go away: the headlines and photographs, the innuendo I know you would hate. With my guidance, you would be back in control of your life, telling the story on your terms."

"What about the police?"

"Ah," he said. "I have an idea for you about the police that I think might work very well. But first, why don't we go and have something to eat? We can relax a little, and I will explain my proposal in detail."

Chapter 49

As usual, the Inspector was the essence of good manners. "Thank you so much for coming to see me, Sergeant. I know how busy you are."

The summons had been an order, of course. But the Inspector always addressed his officers as though they were fellow professionals, rather than subordinates. It was one of the things Sylvia most admired about him. She sat in the chair he indicated.

"I wanted to bring you up to date on developments in the case of the missing Contessa."

"Thank you, Sir."

"It seems that Signor di Tramonti's current lawyer ... he dismissed the first one ... has applied for his release on the basis that we have no concrete evidence he committed any of the crimes for which he is being detained. She, the lawyer, asserts that our case against Signor di Tramonti is entirely circumstantial and that," he bent to read a document, "her client has been 'the victim of a grave injustice'."

Sergeant Sylvia frowned in confusion. "But the physical attack on the Contessa; the ransacked palazzo; the empty safe; all those valuable heirlooms missing; the Contessa's car still sitting in the driveway. It's all in Officer Paulo's statement."

"Ah, yes. Officer Paulo." They looked at each other for a moment.

Sylvia rallied. "Well, he may not be the brightest on the force, but his statement is clear and unambiguous. I believe him to be an honourable young man; if, perhaps, a little naïve."

"And there we have it." The Inspector smiled wanly. "There is always the possibility that he has been, how shall I put it, misled by what he saw."

Sylvia looked at her hands. There was no implication in either his tone or his words that he held her responsible for Paulo's statement, but she was Paulo's superior officer, and no-one else.

"What do you intend to do, Sir?"

"I have listened to the arguments of our legal team, whose view is that we are on thin ice if this goes before a judge. However, I still believe a crime of some sort has taken place, and that Signor di Tramonti is heavily implicated. Alongside Officer Paulo's statement, we have the evidence of di Tramonti's somewhat questionable behaviour since his wife disappeared." He ticked them off on his fingers: "Assuming a different identify; attempting to sell fake paintings and other goods; signing papers to buy the Spanish villa, and then doing a runner; gaining money and goods from a string of wealthy women. All of which is circumstantial, I grant you. None of those activities makes him a murderer. But add them to the fact that his wealthy wife is still missing without trace, and we have a strong case for continuing to regard him as our prime suspect. Would you agree, Sergeant?"

Her viewpoint was immaterial, but she appreciated being consulted. "Yes, Sir. I most certainly do agree."

"I have discussed a compromise position with our legal people, to which they have agreed. We will offer to release Signor di Tramonti on bail under the usual conditions, with one addition: he will not be allowed to return to his home, the palazzo, while our investigations are continuing. He must remain in the area, and make himself available to us whenever we need him. His lawyer might tell him to hold out for more, but I think he will find the prospect of release irresistible, don't you, Sergeant?"

"I think he will leap at the chance, whatever his fancy lawyer might say."

The Inspector smiled. "And this is where you come in."

"Me, Sir?"

"Yes, Sergeant. I would like you to keep an eye on him. Find out who he talks to, what he does."

"I am happy to do whatever you wish, Sir. But would you not prefer to use someone he doesn't recognise to carry out this task?"

The Inspector laughed. "No, Sergeant. I want the Signor to know he is being watched. It will keep up the pressure on him once he leaves our 'care'. Who knows? He might trip up one day, make a false move. And you'll be there to see it."

Chapter 50

So, it was agreed. Tomas would go to Italy first to make the arrangements. Aurelia would follow when he signalled all was ready for her.

But before all that, there were a few obligations to be carried out. Tomas wanted to take photographs of Aurelia in a range of different settings, "to illustrate your wonderful story".

"I thought you already had plenty of salacious pictures," she snapped.

Tomas smiled his easy charm. "Aurelia, my darling, I will only take beautiful photographs of a beautiful lady".

For her part, Aurelia required contracts, detailed contracts, to cover every eventuality. If any or all of his crazy plans came to pass, she wanted to be absolutely certain she had the final say in all editorial decisions. Even more important, she was determined to make more money than him out of her 'story'. She didn't exactly need the money, but it was a matter of principle that a grubby, if handsome, reporter was not going to come out of this fiasco better off than herself.

Chapter 51

Though it was deeply irritating that he was forbidden to live in the palazzo, Giancarlo relished being out of that ghastly place the police had kept him in. Signorina Domossola had been wonderful, arranging for him to rent a furnished apartment in the town, not far from her law practice. They met often to discuss his case, usually at her offices, occasionally in a nearby café. Gradually, they had advanced to first-name terms. Over time, he hoped she would agree to one of his frequent invitations to take her to dinner, even though she firmly maintained a professional distance from her client.

Giancarlo didn't mind. It wasn't as though he wanted a romantic relationship with her. He had been tripped up by too many women lately, women who were not as innocent or sweet or rich as they seemed. No, he simply enjoyed being in the company of a beautiful, intelligent young woman, and Daniela Domossola was all of these things. He flirted with her, of course; it was how Giancarlo had always related to women, right from being a little boy. He could see that she enjoyed his flattery, even though she was careful not to flirt back.

One day, he hired a car and drove over to Josefina's house, bearing armfuls of pale pink tulips. She was thrilled to see him.

"Come in. Come in. Oh Signor, I never for one moment believed all those lies they told about you in the paper."

Giancarlo kissed both her cheeks. "You have always been a true and loyal friend, Josefina, and I will forever be in your debt."

Josefina plied him with coffee and cakes, and fussed with arranging the tulips in a vase, all the while chattering about the damage done to the palazzo by the police and media types trampling over it.

"I go there every day, Sir. It is all tidied up, and looking spick and span, ready for you to return to whenever you want."

"Alas, Josefina, I am not permitted to go to the house until all these stupid misunderstandings have been cleared up. But I am immensely grateful for all you are doing. You must tell me what you are owed, and as soon as my finances are fully released, I will ensure you are reimbursed."

"Oh you don't need to worry about that, Sir. My wages have been paid regularly by the solicitor, as have all the staff's wages, as well as the costs of any repairs needed."

"Really? Well, I am delighted to know that you have not been out of pocket during my absence."

They did not talk directly of the Contessa, nor speculate on her whereabouts, though Josefina hinted strongly that she had had cause to speak sharply to her husband on more than one occasion. "Giuseppe can be very foolish and easily led by the wrong sort of people," she confided. "I told him: 'Giuseppe, you must not believe all the gossip you hear in the village. They are ignorant people, and will be swayed by any rubbish stories printed in the paper.' I said to him: 'The Signor has always behaved honourably towards his wife, as he has to everyone he meets, and I will not hear a word against him.'" She beamed at Giancarlo, and he patted her hand.

So, the locals believed that he had harmed his wife, perhaps even done away with her.

Returning to his car, Giancarlo saw the blowsy Sergeant leaning against a wall nearby. He had caught sight of her in several different places since his release. She never attempted to conceal her presence, or to approach him. She simply stared, and then jotted something in a notebook. Giancarlo held back a scowl. What did these people think he was going to do? Buy a shovel and dig up his wife's body? It was ridiculous. But all the same, it was a little unnerving.

Chapter 52

The note under Giancarlo's door was intriguing. 'I have news of a certain person whose absence is of interest to you. I should like to meet to discuss this matter further.' There was no signature, just the name of a café, a date and a time.

It could be a hoax, of course. There had been others purporting to know where Aurelia was living, or held captive, or buried. Still others tried to blackmail him in exchange for their information. Well, blackmail would never work since Giancarlo had nothing to hide, at least nothing these strangers could possibly know about. But this simple note was different; it made no elaborate claims or threats. It might be genuine. Though Giancarlo had no desire for Aurelia's return, he would welcome any proof that she was alive so that the police case against him would collapse. Perhaps he should show the note to Daniela? Not yet, he decided. First, he would discreetly check out the sender.

Sitting across the road in his car, Giancarlo scanned the faces of the few customers in the café. There was no sign of the yellow-haired Sergeant. People came and went, but the cafe wasn't very busy. One man sat alone for over an hour, facing towards the door. He appeared to be in his thirties; smartly dressed. Eventually, the man stood up, paid for his coffee, and emerged into the sun. He looked around, and saw Giancarlo leaning against a car. Giancarlo nodded to him. "I believe you wanted to talk to me."

They walked to a small park and sat on a bench. The man's name was Tomas. He sounded neither Italian nor Spanish, but Giancarlo could not immediately place the accent. Tomas reached into his jacket and handed a photograph to Giancarlo. It showed Aurelia, looking ... well, magnificent. On the back of the photo was a date.

"As you see, Signor di Tramonti, I took this picture a week ago; with the Contessa's permission, of course."

So, Aurelia was still happy to be known by her title.

Tomas continued, "We agreed that I would contact you with a proposition that will benefit all parties."

Here it comes, then. The squeeze.

They moved to a quiet bar, and talked for an hour.

Chapter 53

It was a beautiful, cloudless day when the plane touched down on the runway, following the short flight from Rome. Looking out of the window, Aurelia took in the reception party assembled on the tarmac. She waited for the plane to empty, took a deep breath, and formed her features into a dignified smile as she stood on the top step. As agreed in Rio, Tomas had brought along a photographer, and she heard the clicking of the camera as she descended the steps. Tomas stepped forward and kissed her cheek, whispering, "You look like a movie star."

Her eyes flickered over the police car to the side, and he said, "I promise I didn't know they'd be here, Aurelia. They must have been alerted when you changed planes in Rome."

He led her towards a handsome man in immaculate uniform standing next to a female officer with badly-dyed hair. The man bowed slightly proffering his hand. "Welcome, Contessa di Tramonti. It is a pleasure to meet you at last, and to see for myself that you are safe and well."

The Inspector introduced himself and his Sergeant, and the photographer kept on snapping away like an irritating little dog. The glare from Sergeant Sylvia stopped him in his tracks, and Tomas motioned to him to move back from the officers.

"Thank you, Inspector," Aurelia smiled. "I am sorry to have caused you such inconvenience."

"No inconvenience, I assure you." For a few seconds the Inspector looked directly into her eyes, and Aurelia had the unsettling impression that he saw right through her. She drew her gaze away and looked about her, "I wondered if perhaps my husband might be here?"

"I thought you might prefer your reconciliation to be a little more private than this, and I have therefore arranged for him to meet us at the palazzo. If you would permit me?" He gestured to the police car.

"That is very thoughtful of you, Inspector."

She could see Tomas scowling at the thought he might be denied his best picture. Then he spoke to his photographer and they both scurried off.

Chapter 54

Aurelia felt her heartbeat quicken as they drew up outside and she gazed on the familiar sturdy walls covered in flowering climbers. *My beautiful palazzo.* And there was her powder blue Lamborghini, just as she had left it. There, too, were Tomas and the photographer. They must have driven like demons to arrive before the police car. It was all she could do not to laugh. *All these men, hanging on my every word. While inside, my precious husband waits to greet me. This is going to be so entertaining.*

Giancarlo looked different, younger. He had smartened up; it was an improvement. Aurelia understood that, as the supposed 'victim', the first approach must come from her, so she opened her arms and moved swiftly towards him. "Caro mio!" They embraced fondly. The camera clicked away. The police officers watched closely.

"My darling Aurelia. I have been sick with worry about you." Releasing himself from her arms, he took both her hands and stood back to take stock. "You look wonderful. But please assure me you are perfectly well and in no danger."

She laughed gaily. "Oh Giancarlo, my dearest, it is so good to see you. You always fret about me so. I am perfectly well, thank you, and I have never been in any danger whatsoever." The photographer moved to a different angle.

"Thank God," he breathed, and embraced her in a bear hug which lasted perhaps a fraction too long. *Don't overdo it, Giancarlo.*

There was a small cough from the Inspector. "I wonder if we might all sit down? There are a number of details to be clarified."

"Of course, Inspector," and Aurelia gestured to the chairs. As everyone prepared to sit, Sergeant Sylvia went over and spoke to Tomas and the photographer, who reluctantly left the room.

From nowhere, Josefina appeared bearing coffee and cakes, and bustled about, serving them.

"Thank you, Josefina," said Aurelia coolly.

"Madam," she bobbed, and then bestowed a radiant smile on Giancarlo that was not lost on anyone in the room. No-one spoke until she had gone.

The Inspector began by reading out Officer Paulo's report written on the night of the Contessa's disappearance. When he reached the part about the marks on her face, Aurelia appeared to become quite agitated.

"Oh Inspector, this has all been misinterpreted. The cuts and bruises on my face were from the treatment I had been having at a private hospital."

"Treatment?"

"Surgery . . . a small operation."

Sergeant Sylvia spoke. "A facelift". It was not a question. "I will need the name of the hospital from you later, Contessa."

"Naturally." Aurelia shifted in her chair.

The Inspector referred again to the report. "Officer Paulo quotes you as saying that you and your husband had fought, and that he had a terrible temper."

"We had argued that day, it's true. I was cross with him, and may have exaggerated a little to the young policeman. Giancarlo and I have a somewhat volatile relationship – we both have rather short tempers ..." she glanced at her husband, who leaned forward and took her hand. "But my Giancarlo would never lay a finger on me."

"Would you mind telling us what the argument was about?"

"It was a trivial issue, really. I was expecting my husband to collect me from the hospital, but he said he was too busy and had arranged for someone else to take me home instead. I was feeling poorly and in some pain, and I suppose I had hoped for a little more sympathy. The fact that he arrived at the palazzo just a few moments after me only increased my irritation, because I felt he could have made the effort to collect me himself if he'd wanted to."

Giancarlo pulled a rueful face. "I should have made the time. It was not much to ask. I am so sorry for my selfishness, Aurelia."

Sylvia interpreted the small movement of the Inspector's head as irritation with this farce, but his voice gave nothing away. "And immediately after the quarrel. What happened next?"

"I got back in my car and drove away," explained Giancarlo.

The Inspector looked at Giancarlo, and then turned back to Aurelia.

"What about the state of your room, Contessa?"

"The state of my room?"

Sergeant Sylvia said, "Officer Paulo reported a great deal of disarray in your bedroom; cupboards and drawers open, clothes lying everywhere, objects scattered about."

Aurelia looked from one to the other in some confusion. "Is that a problem? I don't quite understand what you are inferring."

"It looked to the Officer and to me as if the room had been ransacked."

Giancarlo interrupted. "If I may just say something here. My wife is accustomed to having staff who clean up and put things away. It is quite normal for her to be a little – shall we say – untidy." He bestowed an indulgent smile on Aurelia.

Sergeant Sylvia persisted. "Then there is the matter of the open safe."

"Yes?"

"Why was the safe door left open, Contessa?"

"Obviously, because I had just emptied it," Aurelia failed to keep the sarcasm from her voice.

"And you would usually leave the door open?"

"If the safe was empty, why would I bother closing the door?" Tired of this woman with the ill-fitting uniform, Aurelia turned to the Inspector. "Tell me, why?"

The Inspector got up and walked round the sofas, coming to stand in front of a delicate portrait in an ornate frame. "Contessa, I should like to ask you about all the fine works of art in this palazzo."

"They are mostly heirlooms collected over the years by my first husband and his ancestors. Many of the pieces are exquisite, some are irreplaceable. Others are worth relatively little, but I keep them as reminders of the Conte."

"Quite so." He gave a small smile. "Officer Paulo states that you accused your husband of stealing rather a lot of these heirlooms. Indeed, you led the officer to various rooms and pointed out where paintings, silverware and other valuable items would normally be kept."

Aurelia raised her cup to her lips. Tomas had advised her not to volunteer any information that might incriminate her, simply to answer direct questions with as little elaboration as possible. The Inspector waited. She replaced her cup in its saucer and looked at her hands. There was no sound but the ticking of a small clock.

"Contessa, we are trying to establish some facts here in order to arrive at the truth of the situation. We have the first-hand report of Officer Paulo, a credible and reliable policeman," (Sylvia blinked twice) "who states that you summoned him to the palazzo, told him that your husband had left you after a violent quarrel, and taken away many items of value without your permission. These are the facts, as stated by the police officer."

"And that's what I am trying to tell you, Inspector. This has all been a terrible misunderstanding. The young officer seems to have drawn many conclusions from what he saw ..."

Sylvia interrupted, "And from what you said and did, Contessa. Do you dispute that you took him round the house indicating where items were missing?"

Aurelia paused. "To be honest, I am not at all clear exactly what I said and did that evening. Please remember that I had just returned from having surgery. I was still a little unsteady due to the anaesthetic. I was also in considerable pain, and had taken quite a few painkillers. My husband and I had had a terrible quarrel and he had stormed off. Josefina was not around to look after me; I was quite alone. The tablets weren't working too well, so I probably had a small drink or two to dull the pain. All in all I was very confused and distressed, and may have said things I shouldn't have."

"So you lied about your husband stealing paintings?"

Aurelia's eyes flickered towards her husband, who said, "Sergeant, Inspector, please allow me to explain. My wife did not exactly lie about that. I did, indeed, take a picture, just the one. As a matter of fact it is the portrait behind you, Inspector. I took it out of spite – I knew it was one of her favourites."

"And yet there it is," said the Inspector, "hanging on the wall. Even though neither of you has been back inside the palazzo since that night."

There was a knock on the door, and Josefina came in. "I thought you might be ready for some refreshments". Trailing in her wake, and bearing sandwiches and coffee, Tomas and the photographer eagerly entered the room.

Chapter 55

After the trays and plates were cleared away, and Sylvia had shooed the reluctant Tomas and his photographer out of the door, the Inspector returned to the matter of the little portrait.

Giancarlo sighed. "Following our disagreement, it took me a few hours to calm down and get things in perspective. Then I drove back here to make sure Aurelia was all right, and to bring back the picture."

"Officer Paulo reported that when he returned the following day, you had both simply disappeared, without leaving word of your intentions or whereabouts with anyone. Perhaps you would explain to us where you went." He looked from one to the other. Giancarlo leaned forward.

"By the time I got back to the house, my wife and I were both ready to make it up; the argument was put behind us. It had always been our intention to take a holiday following Aurelia's surgery, once she felt strong enough. It was a way of helping with her recovery. On a whim, I suggested that we leave that night. My wife was feeling very groggy, which was probably why she agreed to such a harebrained idea. Anyway, we quickly put together the few things we'd need, got in the car and drove away."

"Without telling anyone?"

Giancarlo shrugged. "There was no-one we needed to tell. Josefina is used to us coming and going without much notice. She and the rest of the staff keep everything running smoothly whether we are here or not."

Sergeant Sylvia addressed the Contessa. "You took very few clothes with you. Isn't that a little unusual?"

"Not at all," Aurelia explained reasonably. "Part of the fun would be the shopping trips."

The Inspector got up and stood in front of the empty fireplace, addressing no-one in particular. "Where did you go?"

Giancarlo took up the story. "We took a leisurely drive to France, stopped a few times along the Riviera coast, then on to Spain. We ended up in Barcelona." He looked at the Inspector, waiting for the next question. It would be about the paintings.

"Ah, yes. This brings me to the matter of the paintings, fake paintings that you attempted to sell as genuine, along with other precious items."

The loving couple exchanged knowing smiles, until the husband said, "That was all part of the holiday fun."

"Fun? You were attempting to commit a crime."

Aurelia broke in smoothly. "Allow me to explain, Inspector. As you know, my palazzo is full of treasures". She waved an airy hand. "Naturally, they are all insured. However, many years ago we learnt that the insurance company was not best pleased with our attitude to security: doors and windows with the keys left in them, tradesmen coming in and out."

Giancarlo broke in, "'Somewhat cavalier' was the phrase I recall them using".

"Anyway, they refused to continue with full cover, despite the quite exorbitant amount I was paying them. They wanted the most valuable things locked away in vaults, where we could no longer see and enjoy them. We thought about this dilemma for some time, until we hit upon the perfect solution. We would have copies made, a few pieces at a time, to keep here in the house. The originals could be safely locked away where the boring pen-pushers wanted them, while we would continue to have all the pleasure of being surrounded by our beautiful art."

Aurelia smiled contentedly at the Inspector. He motioned for her to continue.

"So, that is precisely what we did. Many of the things you see about you are copies, excellent copies. Though not the little portrait that my naughty husband took away." She giggled and gave a light smack to Giancarlo's hand, and he hung his head in mock shame. "That painting is an original."

The Inspector looked at Giancarlo. "Whatever the reason for having copies made, you nevertheless attempted to defraud several art dealers in France and Spain."

"Ah, that was the enjoyable part. We loathe art dealers, Inspector. They are always so condescending, talking down to us as if we are morons. So we decided to have a laugh by testing them. It's just a little game for us; we've played it before. We have a lot of fun watching them almost salivate when they think they have a gullible person in front of them who's naïve about what he owns. We mix the copies among genuine artwork. Of course, they always spot the copies in the end."

"You are saying that you have never taken money for a fake?"

"Never, Inspector. We don't need money. My wife has just explained that we have a small fortune locked away in vaults, which you can easily verify. As I said, it was a bit of fun."

Sylvia intervened. "How do you account for Officer Paulo's report of the empty glass cabinets, the gaps on the walls where paintings had clearly hung?"

Aurelia smoothed her skirt. "I have already said, Sergeant, that we were having copies made. But good copies take time, and the insurance people weren't prepared to wait. So we had to lock away many items which we intended to have copied later." She looked at the Inspector. "This can all be checked with the insurance company."

The Inspector inclined his head slightly. "Tell us what happened in Spain."

The Contessa looked at her husband and said, "Well, I'm afraid we had a difference of opinion."

"Would you mind elaborating?"

Aurelia sighed. "I admit I no longer care for these little games with the dealers. It seems to me rather a juvenile way to have fun, and I told my husband so."

"You quarrelled about the art dealers?"

"Yes. And about the villa."

"This would be the villa that Signor di Tramonti attempted to buy."

"If I may explain," said Giancarlo. "Quite simply, I fell in love with that part of Spain, its wildness, the emerald mountains, an impossibly blue sea. All so different from this place."

Sylvia's gaze took in the exquisite room, ornate glass doors open onto beautiful gardens. *It is beyond perfect right here. What more do these people want?*

"And on one of my drives out I came across a villa in just the right spot, with wonderful views. I thought it would make a perfect holiday retreat, and put a deposit on it straight away. But when I got back to the hotel and told my wife, she was furious."

"I don't care to spend my life on a mountain top miles from anywhere," said Aurelia. "Nor do I care for my husband making such decisions without consulting me. So I refused to put up the money. We had a terrible argument about it all. I'm afraid I told him to leave."

"And did you?" the Inspector asked Giancarlo.

"Yes. I drove immediately to the agent to see if I could negotiate a breathing space. I thought my wife might be persuaded to change her mind. Or perhaps I could raise the money from elsewhere. But the agent brought in his solicitor friend and they wouldn't budge. Told me it was a legally binding contract." He snorted. "Believe me, Inspector, if I've learnt one thing in life it is that there is nothing 'legally binding' that can't be sorted out – perfectly above board, of course."

The two officers waited.

"But when I returned to the hotel, my wife had packed and gone. She left a note saying she was tired of fighting over money and wanted time to herself."

"Contessa?"

"It's all true. I was exhausted by so many arguments. My face was still tender from the surgery, and there we were, driving from place to place. I wanted a proper holiday, somewhere far away, where I could relax, forget about it all, and just be pampered."

"Where did you go?"

"To Rio." She smiled serenely at the Inspector. "Where else?"

Chapter 56

The two officers crossed the patio and strolled into the gardens. When they were out of earshot, the Inspector said, "What do you make of all that, Sergeant?"

Sylvia was, as ever, flattered to be asked by this man she so respected. She never took his impeccable courtesy for granted.

"Sir, their explanations are incredibly flimsy, though just about plausible. But instinctively, I don't trust them. Their answers, their 'reconciliation'; it all seems somehow … staged. It could all be a pack of lies. I don't know. There are still so many unanswered questions."

"Such as?"

"Well, I realise that theirs is an unconventional marriage, but isn't it strange that they haven't tried to contact each other in all this time? And what about the husband's philandering in Spain; looking for rich women to exploit when he claims he didn't need money? Plus the whole issue of the Spanish villa."

"As a matter of fact, I spoke to Sergeant Maria Carmen about the villa. On our behalf she confronted the estate agent and the solicitor, who admitted that the 'contract' was worthless because they had failed to verify his i.d. according to strict regulations. Therefore, the Spanish police see no reason to pursue our Signor."

"Also, Sir, I'd like to know at what point this Tomas character became involved, what he's after." Sylvia sighed. "No, I don't believe them, and yet there is no solid evidence that they're lying."

"I agree with your assessment entirely, Sergeant. And there is another issue, even more fundamental than a lack of evidence. As far as I can see, they haven't actually committed any major crime, either separately or together. There has been no murder, no abduction, no violence, no theft, no fraud. Of course, we could continue to question them, dig a little deeper into their responses, ask our European colleagues to carry out some checks, explore the husband's use of an assumed name. But that would take up precious police resources, and at the end of it all, there will still be no serious case for them to answer."

He smiled at her kindly, understanding her disappointment. "Agreed?"

"Yes, Sir."

Turning back towards the palazzo, Sylvia stopped, enchanted by a shaft of golden late-afternoon sunshine that lit up the warm stone. "Sir, these people ..." she hesitated.

"Yes, Sergeant?"

"They have so much. And yet they seem to be always ... dissatisfied."

The Inspector followed her gaze. "When we return to the station, the first thing I'm going to do is formally recommend you for promotion. You've done an excellent job, Sergeant."

Sylvia's smile was ecstatic. She would follow this man to the ends of the earth. "Thank you, Sir."

"Come, Sergeant. Let us put them out of their misery."

Chapter 57

The police officers had barely departed when Tomas got the loving couple to re-enact the moment of their reconciliation – for the benefit of his photographer. Judging from the pictures, this emotional moment apparently took place by the fountain in front of the palazzo, on the terrace behind the palazzo, in the drawing room, next to the swimming pool, and standing by the powder blue Lamborghini. Tomas quickly produced his promised article, a lavish, colourful spread spanning several pages that was available throughout Brazil, and translated into half a dozen languages for syndication to any publishing house willing to buy it.

For the next few weeks the Contessa and her husband were much in demand. TV stations jostled for the right to interview them, with Tomas orchestrating a frantic bidding war to determine who would win this privilege. Husband and wife were filmed from every angle. Excitable presenters gushed over the Contessa's outfits, the Signor's charm, the palazzo's furnishings. One Italian media company proposed a game show where art experts would come to the palazzo and compete to spot the fakes from the genuine articles, escorted round the house by bikini-clad hostesses. Aurelia frostily veto-ed this suggestion as being "too undignified for words".

Brazilian producers wanted to make a T.V. film of the 'little escapade' the Contessa and her husband had experienced. There was talk of this film spinning off into a twice-weekly soap opera. A director was lined up. Two actors, whose names clearly impressed Tomas, were said to be interested in playing the leads. Neither Aurelia nor Giancarlo had ever heard of them, but the sums on offer were highly attractive, and Aurelia consented to give the project her full consideration. In the event, it came to nothing.

Through all these negotiations, the di Tramontis were obliged to play the happy couple in the presence of an ever-changing audience. But in the evenings when everyone, including Tomas, had gone, the strain began to tell. They argued frequently. Aurelia could not forgive him for walking out on her and stealing her property. Giancarlo could not forgive her for tricking him with the fake heirlooms, and failing to come forward when he was accused of her abduction and murder. She openly flirted with Tomas in front of him and, despite the fact that they had agreed Giancarlo's share of the profits, had tightened her grip on the finances, expecting him to ask for every penny.

He began to feel like one of her staff, having to seek permission to come and go. He had managed to sneak in a couple of lunches with the fragrant Daniela Domossola on the excuse that he had to tie up loose ends with his lawyer, but it should not be like this. He was a grown man, after all. Giancarlo brooded.

In Spain he had had a taste of how glorious life was without his wife's irritating presence. He ached to be free of her. He spent hours trying to work out how he could get rid of her without any suspicion falling on him. If only he could think of something that looked like an accident, with himself far away when it happened. But the ideas he explored – drowning, poison, faulty brakes – required him, or someone else, to be there in order to make it happen. *If only I hadn't tossed that little rat Fredo into the gorge. He'd have skinned his own grandmother for the right price.* Of course, it was risky to involve anyone else; no matter how much you paid them, they could blackmail you whenever they wanted. Much better that he work alone.

Meanwhile, he detected trouble brewing between his wife and the Brazilian. For as quickly as it had bubbled up, the media feeding frenzy seemed to be dying down. Giancarlo didn't much care - it had never been part of his plans. Aurelia, however, had clearly enjoyed the limelight, and didn't want it to end. Every day she berated Tomas, reeling off a list of all the deals she'd been promised back in Rio, and criticising the lack of progress. Tomas countered by reminding her about his syndicated magazine article, the press interviews and television coverage. But finally, he, too, tired of being spoken to like a child.

"The fact is, my dear Aurelia, that the only reason they are losing interest in your story is because you are still alive!"

Giancarlo's ears pricked up. That stopped her in her tracks.

"So, now you want me dead?" she shrieked.

"Of course I don't want you dead. But we have to be realistic. A missing person, no matter how glamorous, who later turns up can only engender a finite amount of copy. However, the story of a wealthy aristocrat who disappears without trace can be milked for months, if not years. Look at Lord Lucan." Tomas threw up his arms, appealing to Giancarlo for support. Giancarlo thought it wise to remain silent.

"Aurelia, unless you are prepared to lower your standards and engage in one of the many projects I have brought you, then I have to tell you that this circus is probably at an end."

Chapter 58

They settled on a book, seemingly written by Aurelia, but actually ghosted by Tomas. He had most of the material already anyway; it was simply a question of bringing it up to date. The publishers insisted on choosing the title, and came up with:

Missing, presumed MURDERED!
The Contessa's story

Aurelia thought it tawdry, but they would not relent, asserting they knew from experience what would sell. The book was to be promoted by a series of short films to appear on television and on-line, and Tomas had persuaded them to agree that Aurelia would have the final say in the editing. She also got to select, and keep, the designer outfits.

This was the best part for Aurelia. She simply held court in her own home while racks of beautiful clothes were brought to her, along with an army of busy young people who pinned and tucked, painted and combed, making her look stunning. Her favourite dress was a clingy, shimmering silver evening gown that perfectly set off her Rio tan. She would wear it for the filming of her slow descent down the main staircase towards her dear husband, who waited at the bottom to escort her to some glittering event.

The first take went without a hitch. Aurelia looked regal, pausing by one of the priceless paintings, and smiling beautifully at Giancarlo as he proffered his arm. Unfortunately, the director was not satisfied with the lighting, and sent her back to the top where she had to stand around while the crew scurried about re-positioning their equipment. The second take brought a problem with the sound. They repeated the scene a dozen times, and always there was something the director was unhappy about. By now, Aurelia's smile was less spontaneous, more rigid, and as she once more climbed towards the top of the stairs, the director called up:

"Contessa, would you mind trying to appear a little more natural? I'm afraid it's beginning to look a bit rehearsed."

Incandescent with rage, Aurelia spun round furiously, and the spiky heel of her shoe trapped the hem of the dress, which wrapped round her legs like a bandage. She began to lose her balance, stretched out and pulled desperately on the banister, but hadn't reckoned with the angle of its curve.

The momentum pitched her right over the top and, under the gaze of the horrified onlookers, the Contessa Aurelia di Tramonti plunged head first onto the stone floor below.

Chapter 59

Giancarlo faced a difficult choice. On the one hand was the Armani: midnight blue, of the softest velvet, exquisite, and perfectly set off by an azure cravat. On the other hand, a black, immaculately tailored Tom Ford three-piece in the finest wool, lined in burgundy silk. He sighed. Black had never really suited him, and yet Tomas insisted it was the required colour for funerals. In the end, they had negotiated a compromise: he would wear the black suit for her funeral, returning it after the ceremony. A decent time later, he would don the midnight blue for the filming of his solitary walk through the rooms his wife used to inhabit. He'd get to keep the midnight blue.

Aurelia's dramatic exit had initially caused him to panic when, turning from the paramedics, he looked round to find the troublesome Inspector fixing him with a steady eye. But it was quickly established that the fall had been a terrible accident, witnessed by several people, and even recorded on camera. It was obvious, even to the police, that Giancarlo had no part in her death.

Tomas had turned out to be surprisingly useful, organising an elaborate funeral which would, of course, be filmed. When the Brazilian producers got in touch, with unseemly haste, to re-open discussions about making the soap opera, Tomas negotiated an excellent deal, far more lucrative than the one proposed while Aurelia was still alive. He also turfed out the camera crew, at least temporarily, fended off reporters, and generally protected Giancarlo from unwanted intrusion.

When Giancarlo finally had the house to himself, he could let slip the exhausting mask of grieving husband. He needed to think, make plans. His mind ranged over the wonderful possibilities that lay ahead, the life he could lead in this beautiful house, perhaps with the lovely Daniela Domossola. Giancarlo sat up suddenly. What if Aurelia had bequeathed the palazzo elsewhere? It would be just like her to spite him by leaving it to a donkey sanctuary, or some such nonsense. Frantically, he searched cupboards and drawers for a will, but could find nothing.

Pondering how long he should tactfully leave it before contacting her solicitor, the matter was resolved by the solicitor himself, who rang to offer his condolences. After the customary formalities, the solicitor proposed that they fix a date to discuss "the disposal of your late wife's estate". They were saying their goodbyes when Giancarlo enquired casually,

"I imagine you will read out my wife's will at the meeting?"

"I do not have the Contessa's will, Signor di Tramonti. I don't believe there is one. We had several conversations over the years where I impressed upon the Contessa the importance of making a will, but she always refused to do so."

"Do you know why?"

He heard the hesitation in the solicitor's voice. "Well, Signor. Forgive me, but the Contessa said she hadn't made up her mind about who to leave it to." He coughed. "I assumed that she had discussed this matter with you?"

Giancarlo ignored the snide implication. Any discussions between him and Aurelia were no concern of the lawyer's. "So, if there is no will, what happens to my wife's possessions?"

"Well that is what we must discuss when we meet."

"Yes, of course. But broadly speaking, what is likely to happen?"

"If a will cannot be found, then under the law all assets pass to the next-of-kin. In this case, that would be you."

Giancarlo could hardly contain the surge of joy that shook his whole body, managing a bare, "I see."

"However, there is a long way to go before that, Signor. There are certain legal obligations, investigations have to be carried out to ascertain the full extent of the Contessa's estate, and attempts must be made to discover whether she lodged a will elsewhere. In addition . . ."

The solicitor droned on, but the only thing to register with Giancarlo was that all Aurelia's possessions - the palazzo, the heirlooms, the cars, her money and jewels - everything would, ultimately, belong to him.

He wanted to dance and sing. At last, Aurelia's iron grip on the money would be loosened, and he could live the life he always dreamed of, the life he felt he'd earned from all those years of putting up with her. And he hadn't had to lift a finger to bring it about, had no need to compromise himself with some dangerous thug like Fredo. The gods were truly smiling on him.

Giancarlo walked from room to room, drinking in the wondrous beauty of everything he now owned. He poured himself a large brandy and sat on the warm terrace, watching the sun sink slowly beyond the cypress trees, and smiling.

Chapter 60

Lost in happy contemplation as the first stars began to appear, Giancarlo was initially unaware of the doorbell ringing. Eventually, loud knocking brought him back to the present. Probably yet more reporters or nosy sightseers. Irritation swept over him. Hadn't he given them enough entertainment? When were these people going to leave him in peace? Well, they could stand there all night as far as he was concerned. But the knocking persisted until, finally, he strode across the hall and wrenched open the big front door.

Outside, was a short, thickset man with no discernible neck, standing with his back to Giancarlo. He drew slowly on a cigarette, looking around as though he had all the time in the world. He was dressed like a movie version of a Sicilian drug dealer, something that might have made Giancarlo laugh out loud were it not for the palpable aura of menace about him.

"Yes?" enquired Giancarlo.

The man threw down his cigarette butt and ground it out under his shoe, nodding slowly. "Very impressive".

There was a pause, till Giancarlo said, "Can I help you?"

Turning slowly, the man faced Giancarlo. "Good evening, Signor," he said. He half-smiled; that is, the half of his face not punctuated by a jagged scar smiled. "It's taken me a long time to track you down. But . ." he gestured to the property ". . I can see it was worth it."

"I'm sorry; I don't quite recall . . ."

"No, you wouldn't. We have never met. But you do know, or rather did know, my brother."

Giancarlo's brow furrowed in an attempt to recollect.

"His name was Fredo."

Giancarlo found himself quite unable to speak.

"I think we have a few things to discuss." The man gestured towards the house as if it already belonged to him. "Why don't we go inside?"

About the author

Trisha King was born in London, and studied with the Open University, and the University of London. She has worked for a variety of organisations large and small, none of them remotely connected to publishing or Italian aristocrats. A doting mother, she now lives on the south coast of England. Trisha started writing stories at school, striking lucky in 1991 with the first writing competition she entered, The Sunday Times short story competition. She has continued writing on and off since then. And, one night, she had a dream ...

Lightning Source UK Ltd.
Milton Keynes UK
UKOW01f2115070318
319057UK00001B/104/P